Praise for Under Caution

"When danger and romance compete for the finish line, there's no time for caution. Stock car driver Daisy Kray may know how to keep her cool in the high-pressure world of racing, but a dark secret from her past leaves her with nowhere to run and the devil hot on her heels. Zoss's thrilling debut is high-octane and sexy as hell."

—Dana McSwain, National Indie Award-winning author of Winter's Gambit

"Lori Zoss delivers a debut rich with emotional velocity and lyrical force. She drives onto the literary scene with the throttle wide open and her novel hums with the tension of high-speed pursuits—both on the track and in the heart.

With elegant, evocative prose and a story that burns rubber from the very first page, Zoss captures what it means to chase something—or someone— despite the warning signs when desire overrides judgment.

This is a novel of ache, heat, and fearless vulnerability—an arrival worth waiting for with checkered flags.

Under Caution is bold, magnetic, and an unforgettable thrill of reckless love and living life in the fast lane. It doesn't just ask you to read—it dares you to feel."

—Liz Ferro, author of Chameleon Girl

LORI ZOSS

UNDER CAUTION

A Novel

PURPLE**PARLIAMENT**

A Publications Division of Growth Owl, LLC

Copyright © 2025 by Lori Zoss

All rights reserved. This book is a work of fiction. Any resemblance to actual persons, living or dead, events, or locales is purely coincidental. The characters, incidents, and dialogue in this book are either products of the author's imagination or are used fictitiously.

No part of this publication may be reproduced, distributed, or transmitted in any form or by any means, including photocopying, recording, or other electronic or mechanical methods, without the prior written permission of the author, except in the case of brief quotations used in reviews or articles. For permission requests, please submit via the contact form at lorizossbooks.com.

More information at undercautionthebook.com and lorizossbooks.com

Cover design by Jessica Adanich

Paperback ISBN 978-8-218-62129-2
E-book ISBN 979-8-218-62954-0

Prologue

"You know, Lucy, you never hear much about knocking people out with chloroform anymore. It's time I bring that back."

Lumen's voice dripped with dark amusement as he spoke over the encrypted video call. Lucy's gaze flicked over his image on the screen—tall, muscular, his curly brown hair tied back. Her brother's intense brown eyes stared at her, their hardness betraying a deep obsession. Smoke from his cigar swirled in the air around him, and his cold, calculating demeanor sent a chill down her spine.

Lucy spoke with concern. "Chloroform, Lumen? Are you serious? You're not planning to—"

He cut her off, his tone unyielding. "Why not? It's clean, efficient."

Lucy read the madness in his eyes—the way his body tensed with barely contained rage. She had seen this side of him before. "This isn't the answer, Lumen. What's happened, it's done. You've got to stop."

Lumen leaned back in his chair, the leather creaking under his weight. His gaze never left her as he took a slow drag from his cigar, the smoke curling like the dark thoughts in his mind.

"You don't understand," he murmured, his voice turning colder, more distant. "They think they've won. They think they can keep living their lives like nothing happened. And as for Daisy Kray. I won't let her forget me."

Lucy's stomach tightened as she stared at him. His obsession with revenge consumed him, his entire being fixated on the pain he'd suffered. His fingers hovered over a small amber bottle on the desk.

"No one walks away from this," he continued, his voice gaining strength. "No one."

Lucy's hands gripped the edge of her chair, as she tried to keep her composure. She couldn't deny it anymore—Lumen had crossed a line. The man she knew was lost to his anger.

"Lumen," she said, her voice tight with worry, "you can't keep going like this. It's only going to make things worse for you."

Lumen scoffed, his lips twisting into a dismissive sneer. "Worse? It's already worse. They ruined everything—my reputation, my career, my life. Now it's my turn to make them pay."

He reached for the amber bottle again, but Lucy's voice cut through, making him hesitate midway. "Don't do this, Lumen. You don't have to—"

"I'm done listening to you," he interrupted, grabbing the bottle. "I've made my decision."

The finality in his words hung in the air. Lucy's heart sank. There was nothing more to say. He had already chosen his path.

"Lumen," she said, her voice sharp now, "You're not just fighting them anymore. You're fighting yourself."

Lumen's lips spread into a cold smile. "I'm not fighting anything. I'm winning."

Lucy couldn't tear her eyes away from him. She saw the darkness in his gaze, the satisfaction in his expression as if everything was falling perfectly into place for him. It made the hair on the back of her neck stand up.

After a long pause, Lucy spoke again, her tone unwavering. "Look Lumen, I won't be there to help you if you get in this too deep. Don't expect me to clean up your mess."

Lumen's eyes flared with anger, but Lucy had already made up her mind. She couldn't be a part of his revenge. Not like this.

Without waiting for his response, she ended the call. The screen blackened, and for a moment, she stared at the space where his face had been, the weight of their conversation sinking in. She had tried. She had done everything she could, but now, Lumen had chosen his own path.

And she had no intention of following.

Chapter 1

The hum of the engine vibrated through the chassis as Daisy Kray's neon green Number 9 car hurtled down the Nashville Speedway. She felt the raw power of the machine beneath her, the exhilaration of speed coursing through her veins. The track was draped in hot, humid air on a late Saturday morning in June. The scorching sun glared off the asphalt, amplifying the smell of burning rubber and the distinct tang of high-octane fuel. It was the qualifying round for the Tennessee 400, and Daisy gunned for pole position, the coveted first spot earned by the fastest driver, providing a critical advantage at the start.

With each lap, Daisy pushed the car harder, her focus intense and her movements precise. She felt the pressure building, the eyes of the thousands of spectators fixed on her every move. Here, she was in her element. This was where she thrived.

"Riley, she's tight in the corners," Daisy's voice crackled over the radio, calm but firm.

"Adjust your line by a hair. You've got this, Daisy," Riley Thompson, Daisy's trusted crew chief replied, her eyes never leaving the monitors that displayed every inch of the Number 9 car.

"Copy that," Daisy said, executing the change. The car responded, thrusting forward, a testament to her intimate knowledge of every bolt, every curve of its frame.

Daisy shifted her grip on the steering wheel, muscles tensed, coaxing more from the car with each passing second. Her focus laser sharp, the world reduced to the blur of the track, and the roar of the engine.

As a young girl changing tires on her father's pit crew, Daisy Kray had risen to become the most successful female stock car driver of her time. Five months earlier, she made history at Daytona, becoming the first female stock car driver in the racing association to claim victory on its storied track. It was a bittersweet moment for Daisy, a triumph that also served as a poignant tribute to her father, Carson Kray, a racing legend who had tragically lost his life in a crash on that very same track six years prior.

Kray Motorsports was his legacy, which Daisy co-owned with her older sister Morgan. Together, they steered the Charlotte, North Carolina-based company their parents had left behind. Their mother, Linda Kray, who lost her battle with cancer when Daisy was just a teenager, instilled a fierce resolve in them both, driving them to lead the company towards success.

"Last turn coming up, Daisy. You need to break 158.1 mph to beat the Number 76 car," Riley's voice cut through the commotion of the pit and the stands. "Corner four's still slick," Riley instructed. "Ease off a hair earlier."

"Got it," Daisy replied, downshifting with practiced ease. Her hands were steady, experienced from years spent under hoods and inside engines. Knowledge forged from loss and triumph alike guided her every move. She could feel each nuance of the track, a language spoken without words between her and her car.

"Remember, 76's time is beatable," Riley reminded her. "Stay sharp."

Daisy sailed through the bend, tires protesting but holding firm, then punched the throttle. The car responded like an extension of her will, surging forward.

"Adjustments are solid," Daisy observed, feeling the subtle improvements Riley had made after yesterday's test run. "Front's gripping better."

Daisy floored the accelerator, and the car bolted forward.

"Come on, come on," Daisy urged, summoning every ounce of speed from the roaring engine. The timer loomed ahead, digits mocking until they bowed to her will, ticking over to grant her celebration by the slimmest of margins as she experienced a sense of relief.

"158.3 mph," Riley announced, her voice triumphant.

"Pole's yours, Daisy. You did it. You start in the lead tomorrow!"

"Thanks, Ry," Daisy replied, the engine's hum easing as she guided the car toward the pit road and pulled in to meet her team. Climbing out, Daisy flipped up her visor, letting the fresh air cool her sweat-streaked face, as the elated crew swarmed around her, a sea of matching green and black jumpsuits.

Riley beamed. "Never doubted you for a second," she said, pulling off Daisy's helmet, letting her black wavy hair tumble free.

Daisy's heart swelled with pride as Big John, former football pro turned racing crew member, wrapped his arm around her. "You killed it out there, boss!" he exclaimed.

Triumph surged through Daisy as one of her tire changers slapped her shoulder in congratulations, a wide grin stretching across her face. This was Daisy's team, her extended family, and they had just conquered the track together.

"We've got great momentum going, especially with Kelli placing third!" Daisy said, unfastening her fire suit, attempting to cool down.

Kelli Foster, Daisy's younger teammate, joined the celebration, basking in the glory of her own first-ever top 5 showing. The two women hugged as a familiar voice made its way to the Kray Motorsports Team.

"Daisy Kray! Crystal Walters from Racetrack Today! We're live!"

Daisy turned with a practiced smile, readying herself for the track reporter's live interview. Fans in the stands turned their attention to the large screens throughout the track to watch the simulcast of Daisy's interview.

"Hi Crystal," Daisy greeted, brushing locks of her hair from her forehead as she gestured to Kelli to join her in the interview.

"Congratulations on securing the pole position," Crystal said, microphone poised into Daisy's face. "How's the car running today?"

"Extremely well," Daisy replied. "We've got a couple of adjustments to make, but the car's solid."

Crystal turned her attention to Kelli as Daisy took her customary chug of Bassett Springs Water—a longtime sponsor of the Number 9 car. "It's been a great day all around for Kray Motorsports as Kelli Foster earned her first top 5 start! Kelli, what made the difference for you today?"

Kelli tossed her shoulder-length blonde hair to the side. "Well Crystal, Daisy's mentoring and support is what brought me here, and the entire Kray Motorsports crew keeps me going. I can't thank them enough!" She then gave Daisy a side hug while being handed her own bottle of Bassett Springs Water.

Crystal's voice turned sweet as honey as she continued her interview. "So Daisy, sources for Racetrack Today tell us you haven't spoken with Jackson Wyatt since Daytona, and considering your history with 76, does securing the pole with him right behind you in the 2nd position feel that much sweeter?"

The story of what racing fans dubbed "Jaisy" added an extra layer of intrigue to the already electric atmosphere of the race track. Cameras rolled and reporters eagerly scribbled notes, hungry for any hint of drama, romance, or rivalry between the two on-again, off-again sweethearts. As irritating as it was to her, Daisy knew how to play the game; she understood its rules. Racing fans couldn't get enough of this kind of excitement, and even those at the top of the industry couldn't deny the draw of the intense dynamic between two fierce competitors. She leaned in closer to the microphone, her lips turning up into a confident smirk.

"Crystal, let me tell you something…" Daisy began, her voice steady and confident. "Jackson…" She smiled, aware of every camera, every ear tuned in. "…Well, he never complains about the view when he's behind me."

Crystal's eyes widened, a spark igniting within them as she realized the impact of the words handed to her. A soundbite destined for broadcast and social media feeds.

"Well, there you have it! Back to you in the studio," Crystal said swiftly, barely containing her glee as she wrapped up the interview on that mic drop moment.

As Crystal departed, Daisy watched the screens around the stadium replaying her comment, already seeing her words ripple through the excitedly buzzing crowd, some cheering while others whispered and pointed. She shook her head, a wry smile tugging at her lips. This was the dance off the track, one she navigated with as much skill as she did the turns and straightaways of the speedway.

"Oh my, Daisy," Riley chuckled, coming to stand beside her. "Jackson's gonna run with that one."

"I wouldn't expect anything less." Daisy grinned, her gaze following the receding form of Crystal Walters.

Kelli leaned in, her voice tinged with curiosity. "Is the fundraiser later really the first time you'll see Jackson outside of the racetrack since Daytona?"

"Yes," Daisy barely whispered back. A fluttering sensation stirred in her stomach, like hundreds of tiny butterflies taking flight, as her mind raced with anticipation at the thought of meeting up with Jackson at the event.

Riley smirked, "Yeah Kelli, you're in for a treat! No fireworks show can compete when those two are together."

Daisy shook her head and kept her eyes on the ground.

"Wow, that bad, huh?" Kelli asked.

"Oh not bad...just sparks and heat. Hotter than any racetrack you'll ever drive on in the sweltering summer!" Riley exclaimed.

Daisy smacked Riley on the head with her gloves. "Shut up, Ry!"

"Oh, come on, Daisy. You just flirted with him in front of thousands of fans and who knows how many watching at home. It's been months. He's been constantly reaching out and even sending you letters. Sounds like you might be ready for a reconciliation. I hear he's been miserable without you." Riley raised her eyebrows and patted Daisy on the back.

Daisy took a sip of water and sighed. "Riley, you know it's more complicated than that. Besides, tomorrow is race day and all I plan to think about is winning."

"Whatever you say, Daisy..." Riley smirked.

As Riley and Kelli walked on, Daisy fell behind, lost in her thoughts. Despite their fight and break up at Daytona, she couldn't deny the strong pull towards Jackson. Their chemistry, attraction, and mutual admiration were undeniable. She was tempted many times to answer his ongoing calls and letters but the hurt she felt after the Daytona race would creep back into her mind and stop her from responding. Yet deep down, as the months progressed, she still longed for him, and the thought terrified her. With everything that had transpired between them, how was it possible that she still had feelings for him?

Riley and Kelli stopped as they both stared at one of the large screens. "Hey Daisy, get your head out of the clouds and look up," Riley called out to her.

Daisy snapped out of her thoughts and turned to the screen. On it, she could see Jackson stepping onto the podium in the media tent ready to take questions from the press.

Out of the corner of her eye, she caught Riley leaning over to Kelli with a mischievous glint in her eye. "Get your popcorn, Kelli," she heard her say. "Looks like we might get a good coming attraction before these two even see each other tonight."

Chapter 2

The media tent buzzed with the eager anticipation of reporters ready to dissect every word. Fluorescent lights hummed overhead, casting a harsh glow on the assembled journalists whose laptops and cameras cluttered the makeshift tables. The air charged with the scent of stale coffee, a stark contrast to the burn of rubber outside.

Jackson Wyatt sat at the front, a solitary figure against a backdrop of racing banners and sponsor logos covering the walls behind him. Keyboard keys clattered while reporters quietly conferred among themselves.

The room took notice as Jackson's presence took center stage. His broad shoulders filled out his racing suit. A chiseled jaw set, giving him a determined look, as he prepared for the onslaught of questions.

As the reporters settled in, the first question fired out. "Jackson, what's your response to Daisy Kray's comment about you, and I quote, 'not complaining about the view when you're behind her' after she earned the pole position?"

A collective laugh rumbled throughout the room, and Jackson couldn't resist joining in. His eyebrows raised in surprise at Daisy's playful jab; usually, it was he who made such bold statements. He wondered if that was a sign that she was ready to talk to him again. The thought ignited his excitement, and he quickly composed himself to deliver a witty response that would keep the lively energy pulsing.

"So, let's be honest, who wouldn't want that kind of view?" Jackson's playful tone elicited a chorus of chuckles from the reporters, who always appreciated his good-natured banter in response to Daisy's cheeky comments.

"Seriously though, Kray Motorsports is a force to be reckoned with right now, and they've had an amazing year so far. But my team and I are in a strong position for victory on Sunday."

The topic shifted to the previous week's incident with driver Tommy Crow. Jackson shrugged it off. "Tommy and I were both coming out of our pit stalls at the same time, and there was some contact. It's not something you plan for or expect, but it happens in racing."

Another reporter chimed in. "But Tommy ended up spinning out and losing valuable points. Some are saying it was intentional."

Jackson shook his head emphatically. "No way. I would never intentionally cause harm to another driver."

A reporter in the front row threw out the next question. "Jackson, taking you back to Daytona for a minute…"

"Do we have to?" Jackson interrupted with a hint of sarcasm. The room laughed as he took a sip from his bottle of Dragon Cola, his long-time sponsor.

"Just a quick one…in that last stage of the race you ran out of gas, which ended your race day, and a potential photo finish with the Number 9 driver. How are you feeling about your fuel management strategy going into the Tennessee 400?"

Irritated, Jackson leaned forward into the mic. "I've addressed this countless times since February," he said. "We learn from our mistakes and move on. We didn't get a full load of fuel into the tank on my last stop because the refueling line didn't fully connect to the car during the pit stop. That's it. It's a rarity, but it happens. Next question?"

Flashbacks from Daytona were an easy trigger to transport Jackson from his usual easygoing nature to a state of irritation and melancholy. After months of reaching out to Daisy with no response, he realized that losing Daytona was a distant second to losing Daisy Kray.

A new reporter raised her hand. "Jackson, aside from the on-track strategies and the occasional controversies, can you share a bit about how you mentally prepare for a race as demanding as the Tennessee 400?" she asked, her notebook poised.

Jackson leaned forward slightly, his hands gesturing as he warmed to the subject. "Mentally, it's about staying focused and visualizing the race. I spend time with my team going over every detail of the track, discussing potential scenarios and strategies. But I also make sure to have some quiet time before each race, just to center myself. It's about finding that balance between being prepared and being adaptable."

A long-time racing reporter jumped in next. "So, shifting gears a bit, can you tell us about the fundraiser you're hosting at your ranch this evening?"

A genuine smile spread across Jackson's face. "Absolutely. Thank you for asking. In partnership with the Tennessee 400 sponsors, we're hosting a private barbecue to raise money for active military families who need support. We've got commitments from all the drivers to attend, as well as members of their teams who can make it."

"And Daisy Kray will be attending as well?" asked a reporter in the back.

Jackson's grin widened. "You all are something else," he muttered, shaking his head in amusement. "But yes, as I mentioned, all the drivers have confirmed their attendance, including the Kray Motorsports team."

Jackson continued. "It's going to be an incredible event. We'll have great food, music, dancing, and special experiences for the families in attendance, including one-on-one time with the drivers. We're thrilled to be able to give back to those who have sacrificed so much for our country."

"And this is a private event, right Jackson?" asked a reporter in the middle of the group.

"Yes, we want this to be a special experience for these families, without cameras and distractions. No offense."

The reporters chuckled.

As Jackson spoke, his thoughts drifted to Daisy once more. Though the fundraiser was for the active military families, he had carefully planned every detail with her in mind. From her favorite foods to the entertainment and even the flowers, everything was chosen as a way to woo her back.

Since their fallout, Jackson played out various scenarios of meeting Daisy again. He imagined the way her eyes would light up when she saw the thoughtful touches he had included just for her. He envisioned pulling her aside, finding a quiet moment to apologize, to express his desire to make things right between them.

At the same time, Jackson braced for the worst. He understood there was a very real possibility that Daisy would rebuff his efforts. The lingering hurt from Daytona was still a formidable barrier between them. Still, he was determined to try, determined to show her that he was a changed man and that he was willing to do whatever it took to win her back.

As the press conference drew to a close and the swarm of reporters dispersed, Jackson's eyes caught sight of Tommy Crow lingering in the back of the media tent. Jackson sensed something brewing with Tommy so he approached him with an amiable smile in an attempt to break the tension and let him know there were no hard feelings, not on his part anyway.

"Appreciate you coming tonight, Tommy. Looking forward to seeing you later," Jackson said, giving Tommy a pat on the shoulder.

As Jackson stepped out of the tent, a sudden, icy chill washed over him—a gut feeling that he was being watched. He turned, just enough to meet Tommy's burning scowl, and the weight of it drilled into him like a warning.

Chapter 3

Following Jackson out of the media tent, Tommy veered off the lit path and headed towards a secluded spot, shielded by towering stacks of tires. Exhaust fumes lingered pungently in the air, while scattered popcorn kernels from the fans crunched softly underfoot. Overhead, the midday sun struggled to penetrate the dense canopy of service tents, casting long, uneven shadows flickering across Tommy's path. The usual clamor of the crowd muted there, pierced by the occasional roar of engines revving in the background.

Tommy reached into his pocket and pulled out his cell phone. His hands, usually steady and sure on the steering wheel, trembled slightly as the phone vibrated against his palm, each buzz a drumbeat counting down the moments until connection.

"Yes?" Tommy answered.

"Tommy, it's time to discuss our arrangement." The voice on the line spoke with a guttural rumble.

Tommy stiffened. His pulse hammered against his temples. Sweat beaded at the nape of his neck, despite the cool shade provided by the tires. He pressed the phone harder to his ear as if proximity could bring clarity to the choice that lay ahead.

"Go on," he managed, his throat tight, words clipped.

"Are you prepared to follow through?" The voice held a note of impatience now. It brokered no room for hesitation.

Tommy swallowed hard, forcing himself to meet the gravity of the situation head-on. "I am," he said, although the affirmation sounded hollow even to his own ears.

"Good." The voice seemed to soften, just slightly, perhaps in acknowledgment of the magnitude of what was being asked. Or perhaps it was satisfaction at having bent another will to its own.

"Remember," the voice continued, "precision is key. Act One tonight and Act Two tomorrow."

Tommy nodded, though the gesture was lost in the void between them. "Yes, I know what to do."

"I needn't remind you of the consequences should you deviate from the plan," the voice threatened.

The warning slithered into his mind, coiled there like a viper. Tommy fought to keep his breathing steady, to control the tremor in his fingers. He couldn't afford to show any cracks, not now.

"Got it," he replied, his tone steady, betraying none of the turmoil that churned within. "And my family?" His heart hammered against his ribs.

"They are provided for. Your medical debts are taken care of, their futures secure." The assurance was firm and absolute.

"Okay." The word was a quiet surrender, a single syllable carrying the burden of his world.

"Remember, failure is not an option." There was a finality in the voice that brooked no argument.

"Understood." Tommy conceded, the distant voices of the spectators reaching him as if from another world. His family would want for nothing. He'd make sure of it.

"Good luck, Tommy." The call ended abruptly.

Tommy lingered in the quiet, the suffocating silence amplifying the rapid drumbeat of his heart. He turned the phone over in his hand, its weight anchoring him in the reality of his looming fate. Although the call ended, the voice's demands still echoed in his mind. He recalled the chilling moment he realized just how vulnerable he was—the moment the man on the other end of the line first revealed his possession of Tommy's deepest secrets. It had been a normal evening three weeks ago when his phone rang with an unknown number. Expecting a routine call, Tommy was blindsided by the caller's opening words.

"Mr. Crow, I believe you have been keeping some very serious matters to yourself. Matters that neither your family nor your sponsors are aware of." The man's voice was cold, calculated.

Frozen, Tommy had listened in horror as the caller detailed not just his health condition—the inoperable brain tumor that he had concealed from everyone—but also his spiraling debt from gambling.

"You see, I have access to your medical and financial records," the voice had continued, a statement that sent a shiver down Tommy's spine. "Modern technology makes it quite easy to find the perfect candidate for... certain opportunities."

The revelation that someone had hacked into his private records, viewing the confidential details of his life, had left Tommy feeling exposed and desperate. The caller had crafted a noose out of Tommy's secrets, pulling it tight with every word.

"Now, let's discuss how you can make this situation beneficial for both of us," the voice proposed. It was an offer laced with menace and promise. Tommy, backed into a corner by his circumstances and the threat of exposure, had felt compelled to agree.

Standing next to the tire stacks, Tommy was acutely aware of the bind he was in. The man had not chosen him by chance; instead, he saw Tommy as the perfect pawn—vulnerable, desperate, and capable. The plan he had devised for him exploited his situation to the fullest, promising security for his family in exchange for his cooperation.

"I needn't remind you of the consequences should you deviate from the plan," the voice had warned earlier. The threat was clear: comply or face the ruinous exposure of his secrets.

Tommy closed his eyes for a moment, steadying his breath. When he reopened them, his resolve was firm. He had no choice but to play along. With the world on his shoulders, Tommy steeled himself for what was to come, the echo of the voice still ringing in his ears, a haunting reminder of the pact sealed by vulnerabilities.

As he prepared to leave the spot behind the tires, his phone vibrated once more. The screen flashed an unknown number, and a chill ran down his spine as he answered.

"Just remember, Tommy," the voice hissed. "You have no other options."

Chapter 4

Daisy's boots crunched on the gravel as she stepped out of her car, Riley following suit from the passenger side. Daisy's knees were shaky. Her heart skipped with each step closer to Jackson. As she approached the house, she scanned his estate, which sprawled before her in all its rustic grandeur against the setting sun. The property's eighty acres spanned lush hills and dense forests, with horses roaming open fields. Seeing them now evoked a flood of memories: sunrise horse rides and sunset walks, hands entwined, ending with nights by the fire.

Daisy paused for a moment, letting the warm breeze play with strands of her hair escaping the pins of her partial updo. Her emerald green sundress, held together by a petite clasp at the halter neckline, accentuated her creamy skin and brought out the same brilliant hue in her sparkling eyes.

Sporting her trademark red pixie haircut, hip-hugger jeans, and a tightly tucked white blouse, Riley walked with Daisy past the gates and on to the Wyatt Ranch for the fundraiser. Riley couldn't help but notice the featured menu items and decor that adorned the event.

"Look at this, Daisy," Riley said, gesturing at the scene with a broad smile. "It's all for you."

All of Daisy's favorites were on display. Yellow roses adorned with violets crowned every table. Red gerbera daisies lined the walkways that wound throughout the yard. The smoky scent of steak filets sizzled on grilles. A guitar strummed a familiar tune, the notes drifting through the air—her favorite local Nashville band crooning country songs that tugged at her memories. A strawberry ice cream stand serving up treats was a popular spot for the kids.

Daisy smiled, her heart swelling in appreciation for the thoughtful details even as she could feel a light sweat breaking out on her skin in reaction to the uncertainty about the evening's unfolding events.

Trying to redirect Riley, Daisy changed the subject as they walked to a table serving lemonade. "Riley, when is Kelli planning to be here?"

Riley handed Daisy a glass of lemonade garnished with a strawberry dangling on the rim. "Her parents were just getting into Nashville today and she wanted to bring them along. They should be here soon. She's been dying to come out here."

"Why's that?" Daisy asked as she took a sip of the lemonade. It was the perfect balance of sweet and sour.

"She's expecting fireworks between you and Jackson—I might've hinted at your undeniable chemistry." Riley snickered as she walked away from Daisy to greet some of the other crew chiefs.

Shaking her head, Daisy navigated through the throng of guests, her sundress rustling softly amid the hum of conversation. Military families clustered in groups, their laughter rising above the music. A little girl, no older than seven, tugged at her sundress. Daisy crouched down, her smile genuine as she listened to the child's excited chatter about seeing a real race car driver.

"Can I get your picture?" the girl beamed, holding up a smartphone much too large for her small hands.

"Of course," Daisy replied, positioning herself beside the eager fan, her posture relaxed yet poised. As the celebration went on, Daisy found herself more and more at ease in the bustling event. She had always been comfortable around people and her natural charisma and warmth made her a hit with the crowd.

She enjoyed meeting the families and hearing about their loved ones who had sacrificed so much being in active service. She posed for more photos, signed autographs with a flourish, and did the two-step with a couple of military husbands whose wives bravely served in the medical core overseas. She exchanged pleasantries with other drivers and their significant others who were all excited for the race but very happy to be at the event for now, supporting military families.

All the while, Daisy's gaze whirled through the crowd, searching. Jackson was nowhere to be found. She shook off the feeling, refocusing her attention on a young boy who was shyly extending a model car for her to sign.

"Keep dreaming big," she encouraged, handing back the toy with a wink.

"Thank you, Miss Daisy!" he exclaimed, his grin spreading ear to ear as he scampered off.

As the band began a lively southern number, Daisy's gaze cut through the crowd and she caught sight of Joe Wyatt, Jackson's father, affectionately known to Daisy as "Papa Joe." The lines on his face mapped years of sunbaked smiles, each crease a testament to days spent under the unforgiving glare of racetrack lights and a bar fight or two. He stood over six feet tall with a full head of rich gray hair and a matching beard.

"Daisy Darlin'!" he boomed, his voice deep and rich.

In an instant, Daisy was enveloped in his bear-like embrace, the scent of musk cologne with the faintest hint of rosewood wrapped around her.

"Look at you, all dressed up like summer's first day," Papa Joe said, stepping back but keeping his hands on her shoulders as if afraid she'd vanish. His eyes, the color of faded denim, sparkled with pride.

"Thanks, Papa Joe," Daisy replied, her voice catching just a bit. He had that effect on her, always had, especially since her own father's passing.

"Your driving this season, it's something else." His words were simple, but they carried his experience and his respect.

"Means a lot coming from you," Daisy said with a smile, as she tucked a stray wave of dark hair behind her ear. She was filled with the warmth of admiration.

"Your daddy would've been proud, no doubt." Papa Joe's voice dipped with emotion.

"Thank you," she whispered.

Papa Joe's smile faded, and he leaned closer. "Jackson's been doing private meet and greets. He'll be out soon, though." His eyes twinkled with a hint of mischief.

The corners of Daisy's mouth lifted in a grin she couldn't quite suppress. "That so?" she said, trying to sound indifferent.

"Yep," Papa Joe replied, straightening his black cowboy hat.

"By the way," he added, "I think Jackson's horse misses you."

"Is he in the barn?" Daisy asked, a hopeful lilt in her voice.

"Sure is."

"Thanks, Papa Joe," Daisy said, giving him a quick hug.

Papa Joe's weathered hands lifted the brim of his cowboy hat in a chivalrous salute. Daisy smiled at him before turning away, weaving her way through the clusters of people gathered around the property with ease.

As Daisy made her way closer to the barn, the earthy scent of hay mingled with the musky presence of horses overpowered her, as the sounds of distant laughter and music faded in the distance. Her steps slowed as she approached. Before she could step inside, a figure emerged from the shadow of the structure—Tommy Crow. His lean frame was all sharp angles in the twilight, his hair slicked back in his signature style.

"Hey, Daisy," Tommy called out, forcing a grin that didn't quite reach his eyes.

"Tommy," she replied with a nod, her stride slowing but never halting.

"Pole position's no small feat," he said, shuffling on his feet, an unusual jitteriness about him. "Got to admit, you've got skills."

"Appreciate it." Daisy tilted her head slightly, noting his fidgeting hands. "You okay, Tommy?"

"Me?" He chuckled nervously. "Just... eager for tomorrow. Need a good showing, you know?"

"Understood," Daisy said, offering a supportive smile. "You'll do great."

"Hope so." Tommy's gaze lingered on her, a flicker of something unreadable passing through his expression.

"Good luck out there and my best to Tami and your family," she finished with a smile, turning away to continue her walk into the barn.

"Thanks, Daisy," Tommy called after her, his voice barely carrying over the rustle of leaves in the gentle breeze. His shadow loomed long behind him as Daisy's footsteps faded into the distance.

Putting the exchange with Tommy out of her mind, Daisy entered the barn, its familiar structure a silhouette against the evening sky. The straw-covered ground made a rustling sound as her boots kicked forward. Each step brought her closer to the past.

Last time I was here, Jackson and I were different people, Daisy thought, pausing at the entrance, her hand resting on the weathered wood of a barn door. *Those were easier times, before the races were about more than just winning, before every decision felt like a mile on a fast track.*

The door creaked as she pushed it open, the hinges complaining softly. Inside, the barn was dimly lit, and the evening twilight filtered through cracks in the walls, casting long lines across the dirt floor. The horses shifted in their stalls, their soft nickers a comforting background to her swirling thoughts.

Jackson used to say this place was our escape, a world away from the noise, Daisy mused, her eyes adjusting to the dim interior as she moved deeper into the barn. *But can you ever really escape your past? Or does it just bide its time, waiting for the right moment to race back into your life?*

As Daisy approached Jackson's horse Chief, he looked up, his familiar gaze pulling at a heartstring she thought was well-guarded. She reached out, her fingers brushing through his mane, the coarse hairs sliding through her touch like time slipping through her fingers.

"Aw, Chief, I wish we could go back," Daisy spoke softly, a bittersweet grimace spreading across her face as Chief nuzzled her palm. *Back then, it was all laughter and late nights by the fire, talking about where we'd go, not just on the map, but with each other. And now?* Daisy's heart clenched. "Now, I'm here wondering if every sweet word was just another lap in a race where no one really wins."

A rustle at the entrance snapped her from her reverie. Daisy turned, stiffening instinctively as the silhouette of Jackson Wyatt appeared. Just like in her memories.

Is it possible to forgive the past? To start over? The questions hung silently in the air between heartbeats, as her gaze found his. For a moment, it was just like it used to be—just Daisy, Jackson, and the quiet understanding that had always connected them.

Jackson's crisp white cowboy shirt with its top buttons undone revealed a tantalizing glimpse of his bronzed chest. His sleeves rolled up, showing off tanned forearms radiating strength. His blue jeans hugged his muscular frame as a hefty belt buckle caught the dying light. His light brown hair, wavy and tousled, fell just over his forehead, highlighting his striking features. His piercing blue eyes seemed to light up the barn while his five o'clock shadow only added to his ruggedly handsome appearance.

Daisy felt the air shift as he entered the barn, her skin prickling with awareness. There was no mistaking the chemistry between them, silent and powerful as ever. At that moment, she could read it all on Jackson's face—the love, the regret for Daytona, the undeniable pull she exerted on him, drawing him closer without a single word.

He stared her up and down.

"That dress, Daisy. You look absolutely stunning," he said, his voice cutting through the silence of the barn, velvety and smooth. Jackson made his way towards her. Each stride seemed to match the thumping in her chest.

"Thank you," she replied softly, locking eyes with him.

Jackson reached out, his hand tentatively extending towards her. Daisy's breath caught again, this time audibly. The space between them charged with the electricity of their shared past, pulling them into an orbit dictated by heartbeats and hushed breaths. The complexity of their history was palpable, hanging heavily in the air as they navigated the proximity that once came so naturally.

Daisy swallowed hard, her pulse echoing loudly in her ears, a rhythmic reminder of the stakes now between them. Jackson's arms engulfed her in a warm embrace. Despite her confusion and hesitation, she surrendered to his hold, feeling herself melt against him. The warmth radiating from his chest seeped into her skin, like a soothing balm.

Together, they breathed in perfect synchronicity, momentarily forgetting the painful divide that Daytona had carved between them.

"Chief missed you," Jackson said, stepping back but not too far. His hand lingered on her arm as if he couldn't bear to break contact completely.

"Is that so?" Daisy cocked her head, allowing a small smile. "Or is it just his way of asking for more treats?"

"Could be both." Jackson's eyes crinkled at the corners. "You always did spoil him."

"Guilty as charged." She chuckled, her voice light but fraught with nerves.

"Speaking of charges..." Jackson tilted his head, the shadow of a smirk on his lips. "Heard the press got a kick out of our post-qualifier banter. Gotta say, I was pleasantly surprised that you started it."

"Can't let you have all the limelight," she shot back, her grin mirroring his.

"Never could, Daisy." Jackson shrugged, feigning resignation.

The atmosphere of small talk dissipated, replaced by a palpable heaviness. Daisy followed his eyes as they looked at the ground. Jackson took a moment before speaking. She could see he needed to choose his words carefully.

"Listen, Daisy. My mind is racing right now. I can't begin to apologize enough for what I did and didn't do. I've made mistakes that I really regret. The way I acted at

Daytona…" He paused. "It was inexcusable and I know I hurt you. I'm so sorry."

Daisy's throat tightened with a suffocating grip as waves of emotion flooded over her. She wanted to speak, to lash out at him, but his remorseful expression held her captive in its powerful presence. She was drowning in a sea of conflicting feelings, struggling to find her voice amid the chaos of his intense gaze. Confusion mingled with longing, and each breath fanned the heat that neither could deny.

Jackson's hand hovered before it made contact, the pads of his fingers tracing the line of Daisy's cheekbone. "I've missed you so much." His voice rumbled low, vibrating through her.

Daisy remained silent and still. Her eyes locked with his, reflecting an array of emotions she couldn't name. His touch was gentle as if she were something precious, something cherished. His face drew nearer, close enough that she could feel the warmth of his breath mingling with hers. Then their lips met a soft press. The kiss quickly deepened, growing more urgent as if each second apart had been a moment too long. Jackson's hand found its way to her back, fingers splaying wide against her skin, drawing her closer. He journeyed his kiss from her lips down to her neck as she ran her fingers through his wavy hair, maneuvering his head in closer to her.

The heat from Jackson's touch seeped through her dress. Her heart raced as his kiss intensified, exploring the contours of her mouth with an insistence leaving her breathless. She felt alive in his embrace, lost in the overwhelming rush of sensation. The world around her faded as she immersed herself in him. Her body thrummed with desire, every nerve ending alight with pleasure.

Abruptly, a distant call pierced their amorous bubble. "Daisy!" The sound was muffled, but it grew louder, more insistent. "Daisy Kray!"

Their bodies parted and turned as one toward the entrance of the barn. Riley rushed in, distress apparent across her face. Papa Joe's weathered features were drawn tight, his eyes narrowed with concern. Two police officers flanked him, their expressions grave.

"Riley?" Daisy's voice was breathless, her chest tightened with sudden fear. "What's wrong?"

The urgency in their faces, the sorrow in Riley's eyes—it all spelled trouble. Trouble inching closer, ready to shatter the fragile peace of the evening.

The officers shifted, a silent exchange passing between them. One stepped forward, removing his hat in a gesture of respect, his gaze locked on Daisy.

"Ms. Kray," he said, his words reverberating across the room. "We need to speak with you immediately. Kelli Foster has been attacked."

Chapter 5

Jackson's office was a vivid display of his dual loves of racing and ranching. Trophies and framed photographs of track victories lined one wall, while rustic horse gear and Western art decorated another. A large mahogany desk, cluttered with racing magazines and strategy notes, sat under the soft light of a brass lamp casting a warm glow over everything. The room was permeated with the distinct scents of leather and engine oil, each telling its own story of Jackson's life—the leather from his hours in the saddle riding around the ranch, and the engine oil from the nights spent poring over race strategies and maintaining his cars.

Daisy took a seat in the oversized leather desk chair. Jackson, Papa Joe, Riley, Racing Commissioner Antonio Rivera, and two police officers entered the room, their figures casting shadows on the walls. On Jackson's desk, a large computer monitor displayed a live video feed of Daisy's sister, Morgan, and Morgan's husband, Roger. Daisy wondered if Roger would be needed in his capacity as her lawyer or Morgan in hers as an agent. Both looked concerned as they listened in on the conversation.

Officer Griffith brought everyone up to speed. "Kelli Foster was found unconscious at Nashville Airport, with head trauma and signs of an assault. We suspect chloroform was used." He paused, allowing the gravity of the situation to sink in.

"She was taken to the hospital, where she remained unconscious," he continued. "She's in surgery. Her parents, who flew in from Ohio for the race, were escorted to the hospital by our officers."

As Officer Griffith delivered the news of Kelli's condition, Daisy's mind raced, grasping at the details: *unconscious, head trauma, surgery.* The words echoed in her head like a bad dream from which she couldn't wake. *Why Kelli?* The question throbbed in her temples. Kelli, with her relentless enthusiasm and ever-present smile, didn't deserve this. The image of Kelli, always so vibrant and full of life, lying motionless in a sterile hospital room, twisted Daisy's gut with fear.

Officer Griffith cleared his throat, readying himself to reveal the next piece of news. "There's more, Ms. Kray." Officer Griffith showed Daisy his phone with a picture of

Kelli unconscious, a bouquet of daisies ominously placed beside her. "These weren't just flowers—they were a message for you."

Daisy's eyes flickered over to the close-up of the typed message on a small card that accompanied the flowers. She couldn't help but shiver.

"To Daisy...you're next."

Sweat began to form on her hands as she stared at the photo in disbelief. "Oh my God..." she whispered, her voice quivering.

Her thoughts swirled chaotically. This wasn't just an assault; it was a message, chilling in its clarity. The bouquet of daisies—her namesake—placed ominously next to an unconscious friend wasn't just a threat; it was a declaration of intent. Someone was trying to reach her, to rattle her. And it was working.

Jackson snatched the phone from Daisy to see the picture for himself. She could see his emotions were running high, and he struggled to keep them in check.

"Officer Griffith," Jackson's voice was low, but the edge was unmistakable as he locked eyes with the lawman, "You listen to me carefully. I want every resource available on this. I don't care if you have to call in every damn favor from here to Timbuktu, but you find out who did this. And you find them fast."

"We're doing everything we can to find out who's responsible," Officer Griffith replied. "Since airports are considered federal jurisdiction and considering the high profile nature of those involved, the FBI is taking over the investigation. They're already at the airport. Agent Rebecca Turner from their Nashville office is at the hospital now. She has requested that Daisy be escorted there to speak with her."

Morgan's face crumpled onscreen with fear, and concern for her sister sprung through Daisy. Desperate to keep her sister safe, Morgan urged Roger to fly out immediately to be with Daisy.

"Please, Roger," Morgan pleaded, her voice strained. "I can't stand thinking she's in danger."

Daisy shook her head, feeling the weight of her sister's worry. "Morgan, he can't come. You're in the seventh month of a high-risk pregnancy. Roger needs to stay with you, not me. You need him more than I do right now."

Morgan's expression hardened, her tone firm despite the obvious stress. "Daisy, listen to me. You may not want him there, but I want him with you. You're going to be dealing with too much out there, and I can't rest easy knowing you're alone, especially with everything that's going on. I'll feel better and less stressed with him there. And as your older sister and your manager, what I say goes."

Daisy sighed, knowing she was defeated. She bit her lip, conceding. "Alright, Morgan. I know when I'm beaten."

Daisy could hear the hesitation in Roger's voice but the urgency in Morgan's voice won out, and he agreed to make the quick flight from North Carolina to Nashville. "Daisy, I can charter a flight and fly out later tonight. I'll be there soon."

Papa Joe got up from his chair and placed a supportive hand on Daisy's shoulder as his eyes fixed on racing Commissioner Rivera. "So Tony, what's the word from the racing association on this?"

Commissioner Rivera let out a heavy sigh. "Well, no decision has been made yet in terms of tomorrow's race. This is uncharted territory for us. We were waiting for an update on Kelli's condition."

Daisy's shock began to wear off, as a growing look of determination took over. "I want to see Kelli."

"Of course," Officer Griffith nodded, "let's get you to the hospital."

As Daisy arose from her chair, Jackson reached out to grasp Daisy's hand gently, his touch grounding her immediately.

"Commissioner, can you join Riley to gather my crew and Kelli's crew to update them on what's going on and ask them if they've seen or heard anything suspicious? They might know something we don't," Daisy instructed, her voice firm. Officer Griffith gestured for the other officer to join Riley and Commissioner Rivera.

"Will do," Riley replied, hugging Daisy tight before leaving the office.

"Daisy, I'll make the final rounds to start escorting people out of the party tonight." Papa Joe volunteered as he kissed Daisy on the forehead.

"And by the way, I don't know who the hell is doing this but they're about a few bricks short of a full load to mess with you," Papa Joe added, trying to bring some levity to the situation. Daisy smiled at his comforting words.

"Daisy, Roger is already packing. I'll keep you posted on his flight. And call me after you see Kelli! I love you so much little sis!" Morgan fought back tears as she began to end her side of the call. Daisy put on a big smile for the screen.

"I love you too, Morgan! I also would love if you got off this call and rested so I don't need to worry about you going into early labor!" Daisy appreciated Morgan's wink of reassurance as the screen faded to black.

As Officer Griffith directed Daisy toward the door, Jackson stepped forward, his blue eyes looking at Daisy with concern. "I want to come with her."

"Sorry," Officer Griffith replied, a note of apology in his tone. "Agent Turner has given strict orders that Daisy is to go alone."

Daisy took note of Jackson's eyes, which darkened with frustration. She knew he wanted to keep Daisy in his sight, to safeguard her from whatever danger loomed. Touched by his concern, she reached for his hand.

"It's okay, Jackson," she reassured him, giving his fingers a gentle squeeze. "I'll be fine. Promise."

He hesitated for a moment, then gestured for her to wait. Retrieving his leather bomber jacket that hung in his office closet, he draped it over her shoulders, shielding her from the coming chill of the night air. As she turned to leave, Daisy leaned in and pressed a soft kiss to his cheek, the warmth of his skin lingering on her lips as she pulled away.

"Daisy," Jackson interrupted, his voice thick with unspoken emotion.

She paused, turning back to face him. The look in his eyes spoke volumes—worry, love, but most of all, a fierce determination to keep her safe. Daisy nodded, understanding the depth of his feelings for her without needing words. "I know, Jackson," she murmured, her own eyes echoing his resolve. "I know."

With a final, silent exchange of strength and tenderness, Daisy left the room with Officer Griffith, each step taking her closer to answers and, perhaps, danger.

Chapter 6

Daisy entered Kelli's hospital room, and the heart monitor beside the bed beeped steadily, its persistent rhythm reminding Daisy of the fragility of life. The sterile scent of disinfectant lingered in the air, mingling with the faint, underlying aroma of freshly laundered sheets. Soft, artificial light spilled from overhead fixtures, casting a pale glow that barely touched the corners of the room. Outside, the gentle murmur of the hospital's night-time activity drifted in—a distant clatter of a medical cart, the muted steps of nurses' shoes against polished linoleum, and the occasional murmur of voices discussing medical details in low, professional tones.

Kelli lay still, her breathing shallow but even, the rise and fall of her chest just noticeable beneath the thin hospital blanket. Her eyes fluttered open, glassy and distant from the sedation. Daisy leaned forward and gently took Kelli's hand, careful not to disturb the IV line.

"Hey there, Kell," Daisy whispered. "I hear your surgery went well."

Kelli blinked slowly. Her brows furrowed. "Wh-what happened?" she slurred. "I can't remember...Are my parents here?"

Daisy squeezed her hand reassuringly. "They're right outside the door with the doctor. And don't worry about remembering anything right now. Your only job is to rest and get better, okay?"

Inside, worry gnawed at Daisy. Before going into the room to see Kelli, Daisy learned from Kelli's parents that Kelli had emergency surgery on a damaged artery in her neck caused by forced trauma from the attack. Doctors ordered to keep her head still to avoid a possible stroke or blood clot. Daisy positioned herself towards the end of the bed, so Kelli could see her better.

Kelli's eyes drifted closed again, exhaustion plain on her pale face. "Mmkay," she murmured. "Thanks, Daze...I don't think I can race tomorrow."

Daisy kept hold of Kelli's hand. It felt small and fragile in hers, so different from the confident grip Daisy was used to. As she rubbed her thumb over Kelli's knuckles, Kelli's eyes began to open again and a subtle smile tugged at her lips.

"Where'd you get that jacket," she rasped, her voice still weak but with a hint of sarcasm.

Daisy glanced down at the leather jacket she was wearing, a blush creeping up her cheeks. "It's Jackson's."

"I knew it!" Kelli teased, her eyebrows raised. "Take it off so I can see the dress." Daisy hesitantly obliged as she could see her embarrassment brought Kelli pleasure.

"Damn Daisy! Backless and easy access to your neck… that had to drive Jackson crazy!" Kelli crowed, her voice gaining strength. "Please tell me you at least kissed."

"Alright Kelli, you're getting too fired up and you need your rest." Daisy rolled her eyes, but a smile tugged at her lips. "Clearly, you're going to be just fine if you're already back to meddling in my love life."

Kelli chuckled, but Daisy noticed her wince as the movement jostled her injuries. "Someone has to keep you in line," Kelli retorted. "Seriously though, I'm rooting for you and Jackson."

Daisy gently moved some hair away from Kelli's forehead. "Focus on getting better, okay? I'll worry about my own messy relationships." The room suddenly felt lighter with Kelli's climbing energy. Daisy admired how Kelli managed to find humor even in the most challenging situations. At that moment, Kelli's young spirit seemed unbroken even with the obstacles surrounding her.

With a final reassuring smile, Daisy stepped out of the room, quietly closing the door behind her. She leaned against the wall for a moment, taking a deep breath to center herself.

"Ms. Kray?" A woman's voice interrupted her thoughts.

A tall woman walked toward Daisy, every step purposeful and measured. With flawless dark skin, warm brown eyes, and hair neatly pulled back, the woman wore a crisp navy blue pantsuit accentuating her commanding presence. As she drew closer, Daisy felt the weight of her gaze, sharp and unyielding, as if the very space around her bent to her will.

"Ms. Kray, I'm Agent Rebecca Turner, FBI Nashville Field Office." The woman held up a badge. "I've been assigned to investigate the attack on Kelli and the threat against you."

Daisy straightened, her heart rate picking up. "Yes, Officer Griffith said you'd be meeting with me."

Agent Turner's eyes met Daisy's, her gaze unwavering. "I wanted to give you some time with Kelli before we spoke. I understand this is a difficult situation." Her voice was firm but not unkind. "I've arranged for us to talk in a conference room down the hall. If you'll follow me?"

Daisy nodded, falling into step beside the agent as they walked through the hospital's winding corridors. Daisy's mind raced with questions and a flurry of emotions but she kept them all inside and to herself.

They reached the conference room, and Agent Turner held the door open for Daisy. The space was sleek, modern, and a stark contrast to the rest of the hospital. White chairs surrounded a smooth, oval conference table while floor-to-ceiling windows showcased a nearby wooded sanctuary and moonlit pond.

Daisy took a seat, Jackson's leather jacket comforting against her skin. She clasped her hands on the table in front of her, trying to still their trembling. Agent Turner sat across from her, her posture perfect and her expression neutral. She reached for the glass water pitcher on the table, filling two glasses with cool, clear water. She slid one towards Daisy.

"Thank you." Daisy accepted the glass gratefully, taking a small sip. The cool liquid soothed her dry throat but did little to calm the butterflies in her stomach.

"I appreciate you taking the time to talk with me, Ms. Kray," Agent Turner began, her voice professional. "I know this can't be easy for you, with everything that's happened tonight."

Daisy swallowed hard, the reality of the situation hitting her anew. "Please, call me Daisy." Her voice sounded small in the spacious room. "And you're right, it hasn't been easy. But I'm ready to do whatever it takes to find out who's behind this and why this happened."

Agent Turner nodded. "I've already had a chance to talk to your sister Morgan and your brother-in-law Roger by phone but I plan to see him again when he gets in town. Sounds like they have a lot to deal with on top of what's already happened."

Daisy took another sip of water as she thought about her sister, hoping she was doing her best to stay calm and relax. "Yes, Morgan is thirty-eight and seven months pregnant. Doctors consider her pregnancy high-risk so the stress of all this is just awful. She's already been at home for a few months on house rest."

Daisy appreciated Agent Turner's concern for Morgan. The agent shook her head in dismay as she pulled out a laptop computer. "Before I get you up to speed, tell me how you're doing, Daisy."

Daisy's fingers tightened around the water glass. "I have a mix of emotions—anger, shock," she confessed, her voice barely above a whisper. "It feels like a nightmare I can't escape. I just want answers. I need to know why someone would hurt Kelli and threaten me." She looked down, gathering her composure.

"I understand." Agent Turner's voice was sympathetic, but her gaze remained sharp. "That's why I'm here. To find those answers and ensure your safety. But I need your help to do that."

Daisy met the agent's eyes, her stare unwavering. "I'll do whatever it takes. Just tell me where to start."

Agent Turner leaned forward, her elbows resting on the table. "Let's begin with camera footage from the airport."

Daisy watched the footage from Agent Turner's laptop. It showed the airport's luggage area with Kelli waiting for the arrival of her parents. She was waiting in the area for ten minutes when her attention suddenly shifted to the janitor's office about twelve feet from where she stood. Kelli strode into the office without hesitation. Five minutes later a man walked out of the office dressed in a janitor's uniform with blond hair, sunglasses, and a medical mask. He carried a garbage bag. He blended into the heavy crowd. Twenty minutes later Kelli's parents appeared on the video looking for Kelli. Soon after, another janitor went to the office, opened the door, and yelled for police.

"Something or someone got her attention in that office," Agent Turner commented as she walked Daisy through the video. "We also confirmed that the blond man in the video is not an employee of the airport and we are certain he's wearing a wig to disguise himself."

The room spun as the images in the video replayed in Daisy's mind. A moment passed in heavy silence before she could speak again.

"Can you pull up the shot of the man coming out of the janitor's office again?" Daisy's eyes narrowed as she studied the footage, her mind racing. A strange energy emanated from the screen that made her skin prickle. She leaned in closer, her focus intense as she tried to pick up any tiny detail that could give away his true identity.

"Do you recognize him? Anything stand out to you?" Agent Turner asked.

Daisy shook her head slowly, her eyes never leaving the screen. "No, I don't think I've seen him. But something about him... it's familiar but I can't pinpoint it yet."

Frustration simmered as she replayed the footage. The man's features seemed just out of reach, teasing her with a sense of almost recognition. She tightened her jaw, the muscles in her neck tensing with the effort to recall where she might have seen him before. The urgency to identify him clawed at her insides, fueling a fire of determination within her.

"I've got a team looking at all camera footage throughout the airport so I anticipate seeing him pop up again shortly but nothing at this time." Agent Turner reported. She then closed out the video to open a zoomed-in photo of the flowers and card that were discovered next to an unconscious Kelli. Daisy's discomfort grew as the image of an unconscious Kelli lying on the janitor's office floor flashed on the screen.

"We're talking to local flower shops to see if they remember selling a bouquet of daisies within the last 24 hours or so. We verified they were fresh cut and still had moisture on their stems." Daisy nodded as she stared at the message on the card with the flowers.

Daisy felt a chill run down her spine as she viewed the photo. Her voice barely a whisper strained with fear, she said, "I just can't believe this is happening. This is all so cryptic, Agent Turner. Disguises, the written threat, and flowers. I'm really at a loss right now." Daisy could feel her eyes watering and took a moment to compose herself.

"Daisy, have you had any suspicious encounters recently? Anything out of the ordinary? Even the littlest detail may be helpful."

Daisy sat back in her chair, her mind scrolling through thoughts and memories. As she delved into the recesses of her recent encounters, she couldn't shake off the feeling that something crucial was just at the edge of her consciousness but nothing solid came to mind. "Nothing unusual I can think of right now."

Agent Turner began to pack up her laptop and other folders. "Okay Daisy, one more thing before we go. The race. I have verified with your racing commissioner that they have decided to move forward with the race tomorrow. Although a threat has been made against you, we can put measures in place to enhance your protection."

"What did you have in mind, Agent Turner?" Daisy asked.

"I've arranged for a security detail to be assigned to you and Kelli. I've also contacted our people in Charlotte who will be with your sister out of an abundance of caution."

Daisy nodded a mixture of relief and apprehension washing over her. The idea of constantly being watched over by strangers was unsettling, but she knew it was necessary. She couldn't take any chances, not with her life and Kelli's on the line.

"So, no one is going to try and stop me from racing tomorrow?" Daisy asked with a mixture of relief and surprise.

Agent Turner half smiled. "Frankly Daisy and I can't believe I'm saying this considering you drive a speeding car for a living…but Nashville Speedway is probably one of the safest places for you to be right now. We can work with local authorities on precautionary measures before, during, and after the race in addition to the FBI's protection. There are plenty of cameras for us to tap into and systems already in place for large crowd security."

Daisy was relieved to hear this as she needed to drive. Not just to go for the win but also because the racetrack was a place of solace and happiness for her, and when necessary, her therapy.

Agent Turner continued as she stood up from the table. "Also, we'll need a list from you of essential people that will have direct access to you day to day. Your sister has already compiled a preliminary list for your review."

Agent Turner passed her phone over to Daisy to read an email from Morgan. All the names on the list made sense: racing team, crew members, and other Kray Motorsports representatives. She then noticed the last two names on the email: Jackson Wyatt and Joe Wyatt.

"Oh Morgan, you sneaky one," Daisy murmured.

"What's that Daisy? Something wrong on the list?" Agent Turner inquired, taking her phone back and glancing at the list. "The Wyatts. Isn't Jackson Wyatt your boyfriend?"

Daisy sighed. "Well, he was. It's kind of complicated."

Agent Turner nodded. "Oh yes, your sister mentioned something about a situation at Daytona but didn't get into specifics. Care to share?"

Daisy was uncomfortable with the question and had no interest in sharing anything about what happened with

Jackson but knew well enough that she had to give the agent something.

"Let's just say he disappointed me in a way I'm still dealing with and I caught him in a compromising situation." Daisy could see from Agent Turner's expression that she was starting to read between the lines.

Agent Turner turned to Daisy. "I understand. Full disclosure though, one of my agents spoke with Jackson and Joe Wyatt as soon as you left the house and I had my preliminary conversation with Jackson by phone but plan on continuing our conversation."

"And?" Daisy inquired.

"I think they make your list, Daisy. We'll talk more tomorrow."

Chapter 7

Tommy Crow's phone buzzed relentlessly as notifications from the driver chat groups filled the screen. His fingers hovered over the device, the shock of Kelli's attack still rattling through him. The group had erupted in disbelief, each driver sharing their thoughts on the terrifying incident.

"Who the hell would do such a thing!" one message read, the words heavy with confusion.

"Crazy sons a bitches out there. I'm surprised it hasn't happened sooner " another message lamented.

"Commissioner mentioned major heightened security tomorrow and the feds are involved." someone else commented.

Annoyed by the constant messages, Tommy threw his phone across the room onto his bed. Although he typically didn't drink alcohol the night before a race, this occasion caused a break in the rules. He made his way to a cabinet in the kitchen area of his spacious motorhome parked at Nashville Speedway and took out a bottle of bourbon whiskey. Screwing off the cap, he chugged the rest of the bottle down. Although he felt close to passing out, in Tommy's head self-medication was necessary. He had made a deal with the devil and his part of the deal wasn't complete yet.

Tommy shook the last drops of the bottle down his throat as images from earlier in the day haunted his mind. The chloroform, the wig, and the pipe. He teared up as he remembered deceiving her into the janitor's office, pretending to be a fan, wearing a disguise, and taking advantage of the young driver's naivete. The ringtone announcing Tami snapped him back to the present moment. Tommy stumbled over to the phone and saw the photo of his wife and young son that accompanied the familiar ringtone. His eyes filled with tears again.

"Oh darlin' I can't talk to you right now. I love you so much but I can't talk to you." He picked up his phone and continued speaking to the image on the screen, ignoring the incessant ringing. "When this is all over, I hope you'll someday forgive me. You both will be better off."

The ringtone went quiet as the call went to voicemail. Just as Tommy started to put down his phone, a text notification appeared from Tami.

"Just heard from Russ Chandler's wife about Kelli Foster. Just horrible! Hope you're okay! Call me. Love you!"

Even a bit intoxicated Tommy knew it would be suspicious not to respond to Tami. She would keep calling and texting until she heard from him so he texted her back with a simple, straightforward lie.

"I'm fine, honey. Situation is awful. With some racing folks so have to run. Love you!"

His conscience required another drink. In one afternoon he deceived his team, attacked a fellow driver, and lied to his wife. Still he one hundred percent planned to follow through on the deal he made to assure his family's future. In his mind, he was in a no-win situation and there was only one way to protect his family.

Before heading back to his bed, Tommy removed a white envelope with Tami's name on the front that was sitting on a small kitchen counter. The contents of the envelope were the only assurance he could think of in the event the man blackmailing him tried to back out on his part of the deal. He carefully placed the envelope in a lock box he kept on the floor of his closet. He then turned off the lights and laid down on his bed, drifting off to sleep as he negotiated with a much higher power.

"Have mercy on my soul."

Chapter 8

Daisy settled into the plush back seat of the sleek black luxury sedan, grateful for the comforting sound of its powerful engine and the supple leather beneath her. Next to her sat an agent on Daisy's security detail. His broad frame exuded a sense of strength and protection as he surveyed their surroundings with unwavering vigilance. In the driver's seat, another FBI agent's sharp eyes darted from one passing car to the next, her athletic build poised and ready for any potential threat.

The sedan glided through the city streets, the bright lights of Nashville blurring by in a dazzling display. Despite the looming uncertainty that awaited them at the Speedway, Daisy found comfort in the quiet professionalism of her security detail.

As they turned into the driver area at the Speedway, a surge of warmth filled Daisy's chest at the sight of her fellow drivers gathered outside their custom RVs. This private space, where drivers parked their homes on wheels during race weekends, offered a sense of comfort amid the chaos of the track. The familiar faces and camaraderie among them provided Daisy with a small but much-needed sense of peace, offering respite from the tension of the upcoming race.

"Everyone here has been cleared by racing security and the FBI, Ms. Kray. They're here to support you." Agent Harrows glanced back through the rearview mirror, her voice breaking the silence.

Grateful for her friends, Daisy managed a small smile as the car pulled to a stop. She stepped out into the cool night air, immediately enveloped by a wave of support. One of the veteran drivers on the circuit reached for her hand first, his grip firm and reassuring.

"We're all behind you, Daisy. Anything you need, just say the word," he said, his voice soft with concern.

"Thank you. It means a lot," Daisy responded, her voice steady but her eyes glistening with unshed tears.

As the drivers dispersed, Daisy walked towards her motorhome, when she heard a familiar voice calling out to her. Turning, she saw Jackson. Her heart gave a small, comforting flutter at the sight of him. The way he moved toward her, without hesitation, spoke volumes—his protective nature, his concern for her. At that moment, Daisy felt an unexpected sense of relief, as if his presence alone could offer a shield from the turmoil that surrounded them.

"How's Kelli?" Jackson asked while quickly closing the distance between them.

Daisy exhaled slowly. "She's stable," she replied, forcing a smile. "Docs are hopeful, but she's not out of the woods yet. She can't remember anything either."

Jackson's brows furrowed briefly, but as the weight of her words sank in, the tension in his face eased. A quiet sigh escaped him as he gave a small shake of his head, his lips pressing together in a tight, empathetic line. "That's tough, but I'm glad she's fighting through. Been worried sick about you both since you left."

Daisy nodded, appreciating his concern. Hearing him express his worry for her in such a heartfelt way made her feel seen, valued. "Yeah, it's been a hell of a day. Got FBI protection now. Feels unreal, but I need it, I guess."

"And how are you holding up?" Jackson, his voice soft and tender.

Daisy's eyes flickered, and for a brief moment, her shoulders relaxed. The hard set of her jaw eased, and her lips parted slightly as if she was about to say something but couldn't quite find the words. She glanced away for just a heartbeat, her hands unclenching from their tense fists at her sides, the armor she'd built around herself weakening ever so slightly under Jackson's steady gaze.

"It's a lot, but I'm hanging in there," she admitted. "Just trying to focus on the race tomorrow, but everything that's happened…"

Jackson reached out and gently squeezed her shoulder. "You don't have to go through this alone, you know."

Daisy's eyes met his, seeing in them sincerity and concern. Despite their tumultuous history, she couldn't deny the comfort she felt in his presence.

Jackson moved closer. "I talked to Morgan and your security team. They're okay with me staying next door at Kelli's motorhome tonight. Just wanna make sure you're alright."

Daisy's heart swelled. "Jackson, that… thank you. It means a lot that you're here."

Jackson reached out, touching the collar of his jacket that Daisy was still wearing. "Are you sure you should be driving tomorrow? After everything that's happened?"

Fatigue pulled at her limbs, and part of her longed to just collapse into his arms and forget the world outside. But a deeper, stubborn fire within her refused to be extinguished. "I have to drive, Jackson. For me, for Kelli. It's what we do."

He held her gaze, serious yet supportive. "Had to ask. I just…" He sighed, stepping closer. "I'm here for you. All night. Just call if you need anything."

Daisy wrapped her arms around him, pulling him into a warm embrace that she didn't want to break. For a moment, everything else faded, and it was just the two of them, enveloped in one another. When she finally pulled away, she kissed him softly on the cheek, her lips lingering for a moment longer than usual.

"Thank you, Jackson. Really."

Jackson's smile was warm and tinged with humor. "There's no other place I'd rather be. Well, maybe one," he joked, nodding toward the bedroom window of Daisy's motorhome with a playful grin.

Daisy rolled her eyes, a laugh escaping her despite the day's tension. "See you at the finish line, 76. I plan on passing you for that checkered flag."

Jackson's laughter echoed back to her as he walked away. "We'll just see about that, Number 9."

As Daisy stepped into the quiet of her motorhome, the solitude wrapped around her like a protective shroud. She pulled Jackson's jacket tighter around her shoulders, the scent of worn leather and sandalwood offering a comforting presence. Tomorrow wasn't just another race; it was her declaration of defiance against the bedlam that had encroached upon her life.

She sank into the couch, letting the quiet envelop her as thoughts of the day's events weighed down on her. The race track outside lay silent now, but it was a false calm, masking the tension and anticipation that hung in the air like a charged cloud ready to burst.

As Daisy sat there, the quiet of the motorhome pressing in on her, her phone buzzed. Startled, she reached for it and saw Morgan's name flash across the screen. For a moment, she hesitated, unsure of how to answer. She didn't want to worry her sister, but she knew Morgan wouldn't back off until she knew what was going on.

She swiped to answer. "Hey, Morgan," she said, trying to sound more composed than she felt.

"Daisy," Morgan's voice was softer than usual, laced with concern. "Roger should be there in a couple hours. Also wanted to let you know that I told Jackson it was okay to stay in Kelli's motorhome tonight in case you needed anything. I also may have mentioned to the FBI that Jackson's officially on your approved essential persons list."

Daisy smirked. "Yes, I heard something about that from Agent Turner and just ran into Jackson."

Morgan's voice exuded a light chuckle. "I know. I know. But listen, he's really concerned, and he wants to be there for you. I know it's a lot, but he's just trying to make sure you're taken care of."

Daisy paused, her thoughts softening as she imagined Jackson's steady presence. "I get it. I appreciate it. I really do."

"I knew you would," Morgan said warmly. "You're strong, but it's okay to let others help too. Anyway, I'll let you get some rest. You've got a big day tomorrow."

"Thanks, Morgan," Daisy said gently, her heart a little lighter than before. "I love you."

"Love you too, little sister. Get some sleep."

As the call ended, Daisy closed her eyes, trying to summon sleep and the strength it could bring. As the night deepened, so did the unease that crept along the edges of her resolve. The pulse of her racing heart mingled with a whisper of the wind outside, a murmur that felt like a warning. The darkness outside pressed against the windows of her motorhome, a reminder of the threat that had shaken her world. It still lurked, waiting for a moment to strike again.

Chapter 9

"Lead changes are the name of the game today, folks, and if you've just joined us for the Tennessee 400 broadcast, you've already missed a heck of a start with just 50 laps in! Daisy Kray's tenacity on the track is nothing short of captivating," Don Triggle barked into the microphone of his headset, his voice sputtering with excitement.

"Right, you are, Don," chimed in fellow commentator Billy Dwyer, his eyes glued to the race below. "But let's not forget Jackson Wyatt and Tommy Crow. They're swapping positions like it's a dance out there."

"Indeed, Billy! Daisy's been upfront more than once, but Wyatt's not giving her an inch. And Tommy Crow? That man is a firecracker ready to burst. Let's send it down to our pit reporter Crystal Walters for more on what's happening on the ground."

"Thanks, Don! I'm here with Doug Higgins, Tommy Crow's crew chief. Doug, can you share your thoughts on today's performance?" Crystal asked, moving the microphone closer.

Doug adjusted the headset off one ear to hear Crystal better. "He's pushing hard. We're keeping an eye on the car's performance and hoping the tires hold up with the pace he's setting."

"Any concerns about how aggressive he's getting with the others, especially with Daisy Kray's car?"

Doug smiled. "Well, racing's not for the faint of heart, Crystal. Tommy knows what he's doing, and he hasn't crossed the line. It's just racing."

"Thanks, Doug," Crystal said. "Back to you, Don and Billy."

Daisy's hands gripped the wheel, her leather gloves squeaking in protest. Her eyes flicked between the rearview mirror and the track ahead. She could almost feel the heat of Jackson's car on her tail, his engine's growl nipping at her bumper.

"76 behind you as usual, but watch out for Crow," Riley crackled into Daisy's radio. "He's playing rough today."

A glance to her left confirmed Tommy's aggressive maneuvers. His car edged closer, paint nearly swapping with hers.

Daisy's jaw set. She wouldn't be bullied. Not today.

The crowd blurred with color and noise, but above it all loomed the memory of Kelli Morgan's attack. Daisy pushed harder, determined to honor Kelli by staying strong in this race. She was good at this—better than most—and she knew it.

A sudden alert from Riley cut through the cockpit. "Trouble behind you Daisy! Cars are stalling left and right."

"What?" Daisy asked, confusion emerging in her voice.

"Stay sharp, Daisy. Just keep going. Nobody knows what's happening," Riley interjected.

"Copy," she replied, navigating the turmoil. Her instincts screamed that something wasn't right.

Cars on the track faltered like wounded animals. Engines coughed, sputtered, died. Drivers swerved, their precise choreography disrupted by uncertainty. She dodged another limping car, tires screeching a warning.

"Daisy, it looks to be just you and Tommy Crow still driving," Riley informed.

Daisy's grip on the steering wheel tightened. She wove through the chaos with a dancer's grace, her car's engine growling beneath her like a protective beast. Tommy was on her tail, his presence an unspoken challenge in the rearview mirror.

"Keep it together, Daisy," she muttered to herself, scanning for any hint of stability on the unpredictable asphalt. She noticed Tommy Crow edging closer, a mechanical predator. He matched her move for move, the gap between them narrowing with each heartbeat.

Daisy's eyes flicked to the sidelines where the flagman stood, red flag in hand to stop the race, ready to wield it. The fabric sliced through the air—a crimson slash against the gray smoke.

"Red flag, Daisy. Stop where you are," Riley barked.

Daisy's foot hesitated on the accelerator before she complied, her car slowing to a stop.

But instead of stopping, she heard Tommy's engine growling louder. His car lurched forward.

"No!" Riley's voice yelled in Daisy's ear.

Spectators gasped in shock as Tommy's front bumper aggressively clipped Daisy's rear, sending her car into a violent flip. Once, twice, it turned end over end, a horrific pirouette before slamming down onto the track. Glass shattered, the sound sharp and crystalline amid the chaos.

As Daisy's car came to a violent stop in the middle of the racetrack, Tommy's car accelerated towards the far end of the track and brutally rammed into a barricade, a defiant act of self-destruction.

The screams of racing fans blended with the wail of sirens, a symphony of horror unfolding in that split second. Spectators rose, a collective wave of terror sweeping through them.

Within seconds, emergency vehicles converged on the spot from all directions. Red and white lights flashed, casting stark shadows over the asphalt. The lead paramedic, a seasoned veteran, barked orders over the din, directing his team with practiced urgency. They moved with precision, unfolding stretchers and medical equipment with swift, rehearsed motions. A small army of firefighters with heavy-duty equipment spread around Daisy's wreckage, ready to cut through the twisted metal if necessary. They positioned themselves carefully, mindful of the delicate operation needed to extract her without exacerbating her injuries.

From the stands, the immediate shock morphed into a low, rumbling roar of concern. Thousands of spectators stood, craning their necks, trying to catch a glimpse of the action. Some shouted encouragements and Daisy's name, their voices a blend of hope and fear. Others remained silent, clutching hands and hats to chests, their faces pale as they allowed another first responder crew to attend to what was left of Tommy's car. The crowd held their collective breaths as the emergency teams worked, their attention riveted to the unfolding drama.

There was no sign of Daisy or Tommy emerging on their own.

Jackson burst out of his vehicle, his feet pounding against the rough asphalt. His mind was a torrent of panic. His heart hammered against his ribs, each beat a reminder of what was at stake. The sight of Daisy's mangled car crumpled in the center of the track assaulted his senses.

Memories of Daisy—laughing in the pit, her eyes sparkling with that fierce determination that defined her—flashed before him. He remembered the first time they raced against each other, the way she shot him a confident, challenging grin as she passed him, leaving him awestruck by her skill and audacity. That same audacity now seemed so fragile, so threatened.

"Outta my way!" he shouted, his voice rough with urgency, as he pushed past a swarm of emergency personnel who moved with practiced urgency. Reaching the wreckage, Jackson's sights fixed on the crumpled form of the car where Daisy lay trapped. The emergency crew pried at the mangled metal of the driver's door, their movements precise yet quick. He saw a medic's hand reach inside, checking for a pulse, and felt a cold dread wash over him. He heard another first responder call for a life flight helicopter.

"Get back!" barked a medic as Jackson tried to push forward. His plea to be closer was met with a stern rebuff, the professional barrier momentarily silencing his protests.

"Is she—can you hear me, Daisy?" he called out, hoping for any sign of response. His voice cracked, betraying the turmoil that churned beneath his rugged exterior. The medic shook his head, motioning him to keep back, and Jackson felt a helplessness that gripped him tighter than any physical restraint could. As he was forced to step back, his mind replayed moments spent with Daisy, their late-night conversations when the world seemed to shrink to just the two of them. He remembered how she'd rest her head against his shoulder, her voice soft and thoughtful, talking about dreams bigger than just racing, dreams that now seemed perilously close to shattering.

"Come on, girl," he murmured, his voice now a low blend of plea and prayer, "you gotta wake up for me." His words were lost amidst the cacophony of sirens and shouted commands.

Jackson watched, his body taut with tension, as the emergency responders finally freed Daisy from the wreckage. They moved her carefully onto a stretcher, her body limp and unnaturally still. "Let me come with her!" he pleaded, his voice raw with emotion.

"We need our full medical team with her, there's no room for you!" a medic responded without looking up, his focus solely on securing Daisy for the urgent flight. The finality of the medic's words struck Jackson like a physical blow. His fists clenched at his sides, the fight draining out of him as he realized the gravity of the situation.

As the helicopter's blades cut through the air, whisking Daisy away to the help she desperately needed, Jackson stood rooted to the spot, watching as the woman he loved was lifted away from him. The reality of the situation settled over him like a heavy cloak, his earlier adrenaline fading into a profound worry for Daisy's survival.

"Dammit!" he cursed under his breath. A mix of anger and fear coursed through him as Agent Turner and her team approached to lead him away from the scene.

"Jackson, we're getting you out of here. We'll take you straight to the hospital. We've already gathered up Daisy's team."

Don Triggle and Billy Dwyer wrapped up the broadcast under the somber mood that had settled over the speedway.

"Crystal, what can you tell us from your vantage point?" Don asked, his voice subdued, the usual vibrancy dimmed by the events of the day.

Crystal nodded solemnly, her expression serious. "Don, Billy, the scene here is chaotic and deeply troubling. Out of respect for the gravity of the situation and the individuals involved, Racing Today has decided not to show the crash site where Tommy Crow's car ended up. It's a graphic scene, and we want to be mindful of both the viewers and the families involved."

"Our thoughts and prayers are with Daisy Kray right now, as she is being airlifted to the hospital. We also extend our deepest condolences to the family of Tommy Crow, who we've just learned did not survive the incident," Billy added, his voice equally grave.

Don picked up the thread, his brow furrowed in concern. "This has been an unprecedented day in the world of racing. We've seen incredible skill and, tragically, horrific accidents. One of the biggest questions we're left with tonight is why—why did nearly all the cars stall out simultaneously at lap 57? Why did Tommy Crow hit Daisy under the red flag and then, of course still speculating here, intentionally crash? We are all baffled and deeply concerned."

"Yeah, Don, lots of hard questions here," Billy agreed. "The implications of what happened here today are enormous, not just for the safety of our drivers but for the integrity of the sport itself."

Crystal nodded, her gaze sweeping over the emptying stands as the spectators were guided out by security. "And with that, we've also received official word from the racing association," she continued. "Today's race has been officially canceled. The priority now is the safety of everyone involved and the investigation into what exactly happened here today."

Don sighed, removing his glasses and pinching the bridge of his nose. "Thank you, Crystal. Folks, as we sign off from Nashville, we're all still processing what we just witnessed. I've been calling races for over 25 years and have never seen anything like this." Don looked to Billy to wrap the broadcast.

Billy leaned into his microphone for a final word, "Stay with us in the coming days as we continue to provide updates on any developments as we learn more about today's shocking events. Thank you and good night."

The broadcast ended with a moment of silence, as the commentators removed their headsets, each lost in their own thoughts about the day's dramatic and tragic unfolding.

As the screen faded to black, marking the end of the tumultuous broadcast of the Tennessee 400, Lumen Ross turned off his 100" television and took a puff of his custom rolled cigar while enjoying the moment in his luxurious Bermuda home.

"We pulled it off," he boasted to himself.

He poured a glass of cognac and raised the glass, looking at his reflection in a wall mirror not far from the television. "A toast to the late Tommy Crow and the power of advanced artificial intelligence. Both performed with perfection on the racetrack today!"

He chuckled after taking a sip of his drink. "Now it's time to focus on Ms. Kray. I hope she lives, as that will make the next part so much more fun."

Chapter 10

Jackson sat alone in the hospital chapel. In the front row, hands clasped, eyes closed, he prayed and reflected. The nightmare continued to echo in his head—Tommy's car hitting Daisy, Daisy's car flipping through the air, Tommy driving into the wall. How could any of this have happened?

The chapel doors squeaked open, pulling Jackson out of his thoughts. Agent Turner approached slowly, holding two steaming cups of coffee. She offered one to him with a gentle nod.

"I thought you might need this," she said softly, her voice soothing in the quiet.

Jackson looked up, his weary eyes locking with hers for a fleeting moment. He accepted one, his hands trembling slightly as they met hers.

"Thank you," he murmured, his voice barely above a whisper.

Jackson slowly sipped, taking in the soft strains of instrumental music as Agent Turner took the seat opposite him, and set her cup down carefully against the stone floor.

"So what happens now?" he finally asked in a hushed voice.

"We're investigating the cars and working with the racing association. I'm leading the investigation into Kelli's attack and Daisy's accident. All agencies are working together to find out Tommy Crow's part in all of this."

She paused, watching him for a moment.

"Jackson, I'm sure Daisy's surgery will be successful. She's in excellent hands. What did the doctors say?"

"Concussion and possible damage to her spleen but they won't know the extent of it until they get in and see it. She was bleeding pretty heavily." Jackson continued to stare at the floor in a daze, trying to wrap his head around everything that had happened the past two days.

"Jackson, I know this isn't the best time." Agent Turner's voice was low and earnest. "I'll back off if you're not up for this, but if you're okay with it, I have some questions about you and Daisy..." Her voice trailed off, giving him space to decline.

Jackson exhaled a shaky breath, his eyes fixed on the flickering candle in front of him.

"Sure," he agreed, though his voice was heavy with resignation. He squared his shoulders to brace himself for her questions.

"Let's start with how you met?"

Jackson's face softened as he reminisced. "I started driving for Kray Motorsports when I was twenty-one. Daisy was eighteen, already deep into cars and racing on dirt tracks during the weekends. The day I met her she was working on this worn-down Mustang GT500 her dad got her. She knew her way around a car better than most guys I knew at the time. She was the most beautiful grease monkey I had ever seen, with green eyes that would see right through you."

"You didn't start dating her then, right?" Agent Turner inquired.

Jackson laughed. "Oh heck no! I didn't even talk to her alone. Mr. Kray had a watchful eye on her and me. One time, he caught us looking at each other. The next day Daisy and her GT500 were in a different garage."

Agent Turner continued. "So fast forwarding a bit, although you had success with Kray Motorsports you left and became an owner driver with your father, correct?"

"Yeah, Mr. Kray was really supportive and we left on very good terms. He helped me make a name for myself in the business. The timing worked because he could focus on Daisy, who made the move into the professional ranks when she was about twenty-three."

Jackson took another swig of his coffee, as he watched Agent Turner do the quick math in her head.

"So you've been racing each other for about ten years now. Tell me what makes her so good?"

Jackson's mouth spread into a wide smile. "She has exceptional knowledge of the car and does her homework. She has detailed notes on tracks and drivers. It's like a science to her. And her instincts in the car are solid. It's like she knows what you're going to do before you do it. She's amazing to watch but frustrating to compete against."

Agent Turner transitioned. "So you've been competitors on the track for a while. What brought you together after all this time?"

Jackson snickered to himself, enjoying the memory. "It's all because of a leak in my motorhome."

Agent Turner smirked. "Oh? Do tell."

"About a year ago my team and I were on the road to Iowa for a race. We were in the middle of nowhere when the electrical in my motorhome started going out. Turns out a water leak was the culprit. Everything started shutting down and we were already running behind for a drivers' appearance at a fan appreciation event. My car hauler was an hour ahead of us so we were stuck there trying to make the repair. Out of nowhere, in came Daisy and her crew. They stopped and helped my team with the motorhome while I went with Daisy to the event. On the way there we talked forever. Three hours nonstop about racing, cars, relationships, our moms."

"Your moms?" Agent Turner asked.

Jackson looked at the floor while peeling the handle off the paper coffee cup. "Both of our moms passed away young."

Agent Turner nodded with an unspoken look of compassion that comforted Jackson and encouraged him to continue. "I remember thinking to myself that I never had a connection with a woman like this ever in my life. She captivated me."

"So then what happened?" Agent Turner pressed.

Jackson could see that Agent Turner was enjoying the story, which also brought him some respite from thinking about Daisy's surgery. But just as the laughter settled, a sudden pang of anxiety gripped his chest, and his thoughts returned to Daisy. He could almost feel the operating room around her, the cold, sharp smell of the clinical air filling the space as she lay there, vulnerable, in the hands of the surgeons.

"Doing the appearance together was like being back in her dad's garage all those years ago. I felt like a kid again, getting a rush of chills when we looked at each other. When the event was over she invited me and my team to a private party she was having nearby for her crew and their families. She brought them all in for race weekend and rented out an old bar nearby with a country band. Beer, barbecue, dancing. I finally got the confidence to ask her for a slow dance. I won't lie, we were hot for each other fast. Each dance turned into a kiss, a touch, a feeling."

Jackson's tan face glowed as he recalled the evening, and he could see Agent Turner was eager to hear more.

"It sounds like you found a real connection with Daisy that night." Agent Turner toyed as Jackson saw her raise her eyebrows.

"Yes Agent Turner, you could say that. Besides the obvious you're alluding to, we stayed up talking until early morning. It felt like we were the only two people in the world."

Agent Turner smiled, then straightened her posture, getting back to business.

"So Jackson, what about your teams? How did they feel about the two of you coming together?"

Jackson rolled his eyes. "Oh, they could see what was going on… most of them thought it was about time. A couple of them were a little uneasy about it but came around. We started seeing each other and kept it quiet for a few months, with our teams helping us keep it private."

"When did the secret get out? Riley mentioned something about Jaisy?" Agent Turner wondered.

Jackson rolled up his sleeves in frustration.

"Oh, I hated that name! Anyway, Daisy and I made the mistake of taking a ride together in what we thought was a remote part of Virginia during some downtime before race weekend. It was a hot day and we stopped at an ice cream stand. Daisy's strawberry ice cream had loads of whipped cream that made it onto her face. She looked adorable. Without thinking I kissed her and wiped the whipped cream off her face. Suddenly, I heard a teenage girl in line shout 'Are you two dating!' Turns out she was a big racing fan and posted the picture on social media. The secret was out and 24 hours later some internet article called us Jaisy."

"Okay, so Jaisy went public. How were you able to be boyfriend-girlfriend yet still race against each other every weekend?" Agent Turner asked.

Jackson's voice softened. "It may sound weird but we both handled that part pretty well. The day before race day and on race day we didn't see each other. We were drivers with healthy egos who both wanted to win. When we were together, although we might have talked about racing, we never talked about strategy or teams. The ground rules worked and we kept what was on the racetrack separate from what happened off-track."

Agent Turner raised an eyebrow, a smirk tugging at the corner of her lips. "Sounds like you two found a pretty interesting way to keep things... *separate* off the track." She gave him a knowing look. "Must've been a pretty successful strategy."

Jackson grinned as he nodded his head, picturing what Agent Turner was most likely envisioning in her mind.

"Until five months ago, from what I understand," Agent Turner interjected, abruptly changing the mood of the conversation.

Jackson took a deep sigh. He knew where Agent Turner was going next.

Agent Turner pressed. "Tell me about Daytona, Jackson."

The memory darkened Jackson's mood but he reluctantly gave in to Agent Turner's request to recall the unfortunate events of that day.

"We were in the final laps of the race, and Daisy and I were neck and neck. Before the last lap, my car ran out of gas. My crew and I missed a fuel connection on the last pit stop—no fuel gauge in those cars, it's all calculated and sometimes miscalculated. No one on my team realized it until it was too late."

Frustration was still evident in Jackson's voice. "I was furious. After my car was towed off the track and I was back with my team, I threw my helmet at my fuel man and lashed out at my crew chief while Daisy won the race—a monumental achievement for her. She was the first woman to win Daytona, and it was on the anniversary of her father's death in that same race. Six years to the day."

Jackson's voice softened, tinged with regret. "Instead of celebrating with Daisy, I just retreated to my trailer. Mountain Whiskey had plenty of whiskey waiting for me. I got drunk and welcomed the advances of a couple of Mountain Whiskey girls. It was nothing more than kisses on the cheek, but I'll admit, I liked the attention—it reminded me of my carefree, younger days. I was just Jackson again." He sighed, the regret clear in his voice.

"When Daisy came in after meeting with the media, she found me with those girls and saw the state I was in. I could tell she was hurt, torn between her victory and my meltdown. It was supposed to be her day, but there I was, making it about my failure. The look of anger on her face..." Jackson trailed off, shaking his head. "I wasn't there for her moment. My damned ego."

Agent Turner tilted her head. "Well Jackson, I'm no psychologist but it sounds like her monumental win and the impact of her father's legacy got to you."

"That's exactly it," he admitted. "In that moment, I couldn't handle the intensity that came with being Daisy's boyfriend."

Jackson stood up abruptly, his body tense as he began pacing in a small circle. His feet shuffled against the floor.

"I swore I'd never do this." Jackson's eyes began to tear and his voice quivered.

"I swore I would never love someone so much it would wreck me." Jackson intertwined his fingers behind his neck as he confessed his feelings to Agent Turner.

"But I can't help it. Daisy changed everything." Jackson declared.

Agent Turner interrupted. "What changed?"

Jackson ran his hand through his hair, as he struggled to compose himself. "I always avoided commitment, clinging to my freedom. But with Daisy, I let my wall down. I had never let anyone in that way before. But Daisy... she made it easy. She understood me in a way that no one else ever had."

Agent Turner's face softened, and a slow smile appeared. "You sound like a man in love, Jackson."

"More than I ever thought possible, Agent Turner."

Jackson felt Agent Turner's reassuring hand on his shoulder. "Jackson, I'm going to go against my usual judgment to stay out of the private lives of my assignees."

Jackson looked puzzled; he couldn't imagine what Agent Turner would have to say.

"It's clear how much Daisy means to you, Jackson, and it's okay to be vulnerable and scared. That's part of loving someone. Show Daisy how much you care and rebuild your relationship, making it stronger than before. She needs you now more than ever."

Agent Turner's phone suddenly buzzed to life, startling them both.

As she answered, Jackson watched Agent Turner's head nodding as she paced back and forth, listening to the caller. "Okay, I'll be right there."

"What is it?" Jackson asked anxiously as he watched Agent Turner hang up and hurry to the door.

Agent Turned paused to answer Jackson with her hand on the door handle. "They found something in Tommy Crow's trailer."

Chapter 11

Agent Turner walked into the conference room at Nashville Speedway, the sound of her heels clicking sharply against the polished concrete floor. She nodded to Field Director Thompson as she took her seat across from him. The weight of the situation was clear, hanging heavily in the air between them.

"Thank you for coming over on such short notice, Agent Turner," he said, his voice calm but firm. "First off, what's the latest on Daisy Kray and Kelli Foster's conditions?"

Agent Turner leaned in slightly, her attention sharp. "Ms. Kray was in surgery to stop some internal bleeding near her spleen when I left the hospital. She also has a concussion. Ms. Morgan is stable and recovering. She was upset when she heard about the events at the race, so her doctor provided a sedative to calm her down."

Thompson nodded, absorbing the update with a silent, grave acknowledgment. "And what's the prognosis?"

"Ms. Morgan is recuperating as expected. As for Ms. Kray, doctors will have a better sense of her overall condition after surgery, but it's still too soon to say for sure."

Agent Turner glanced at her phone, hoping for an update from the hospital, but there was nothing new.

Thompson shifted his focus, opening the folder in front of him and sliding it toward her. He tapped one of the photos inside, and she saw the image of a trash bag, its contents spilling out. A blond wig, a medical mask, a steel pipe, and a small brown bottle.

Agent Turner felt a chill run down her spine as she pulled out her laptop computer. She glanced at the grainy surveillance images on her screen, comparing them to the items in the photo. There, captured on the camera, was a figure in disguise, holding the same objects—a wig, the pipe, the bottle. She didn't need to ask. It was clear. "Looks like our man."

Thompson nodded, a grim expression on his face. "We confirmed the bottle contained chloroform and he knew exactly what he was doing. But there's more to this. Tommy Crow left a note and we need to understand the full scope of his involvement."

Agent Turner flipped to the next page in the folder. Tommy's jagged handwriting on the confession page sent a shiver through her. "Brain tumor, gambling debts, lost sponsorships... and blackmail," she muttered aloud. She paused, absorbing the weight of the words. "Who could have pushed him this far?"

"Someone with the power to control him," Thompson answered, tapping the table in thought. "Someone who knew his vulnerabilities and knew how to manipulate him."

Agent Turner leaned back in her chair, the gravity of the situation settling deeper into her bones. The puzzle pieces were coming together, but she knew there were still too many missing. "I'll get to the bottom of this. Whoever is pulling the strings won't be able to hide for long."

Thompson's gaze locked onto hers, his expression unwavering. "You need to stay ahead of this. We can't let this go any longer. We need answers."

She nodded, her mind already running through the possibilities. "Understood. I'll find out who's behind this."

With that, Thompson stood, and she followed. As she moved toward the door, the weight of the investigation pressed down on her. Every second mattered. The trail ahead was twisted, and there was no time to waste. The pieces were slowly falling into place, but there was still so much to uncover. She would not stop until she had answers.

Her pace quickened as she left the room, and her resolve solidified. The mystery was far from over, but she would keep pushing forward until she had the truth.

Chapter 12

Lumen Ross leaned back in his chair, the glow of multiple screens casting shadows across his face. In his office, zebra stripes clashed with leopard spots on his furniture, plush red carpet adorned the floors, and white leather chairs with embroidered red flames perched around a black lacquer table—a tribute to his infamous racing days as "the Red Devil," a persona marked by his fiery red car and equally volatile temperament on and off the racetrack.

Around his office, trophies from his short-lived racing career mixed with artifacts from his travels around the world. A large portrait of him in his racing days, decked out in his red devil regalia, dominated one wall, a constant reminder of who he was and still believed himself to be.

Lumen's fingers danced across the keyboard with a predator's grace, navigating through layers of digital security with ease that belied the complexity of his actions. On his main screen, the protected health system of Nashville General Hospital cracked under his relentless assault. A smirk played on his lips, his mood buoyant, almost giddy, as he breached the final firewall. He leaned back, drawing a deep breath and savoring the rich aroma of his custom-rolled cigar, as its smoke swirled around him like the dark thoughts that filled his mind.

The medical records he sought popped up on his screen, and his eyes gleamed with triumph. There, in clinical, impersonal terms, was the status of Daisy Kray. He scanned the information rapidly. *"Surgery to stop internal bleeding around the spleen, concussion, stable condition but experienced delayed emergence from anesthesia..."*

Each word delivered a perverse thrill through his veins. It wasn't just about seeing her vulnerable; it was about knowing something so intimate, so private about someone who had become an obsession.

As he scrolled further, a note from the doctor caught his attention: *"Due to the high-profile nature of the patient and ongoing investigations, FBI security detail is present. Any new medical personnel must be cleared with federal agents on site."*

Lumen chuckled softly. "Of course, the darling of the sport gets her knights in FBI armor. How very fitting for racing's sweetheart."

Lumen laughed, the sound echoing in the vastness of his office. "Delayed emergence, eh? Tommy must have done some number on that pretty little head of yours."

A note from the surgeon mentioning that Daisy would be unable to drive or travel during her recovery caught his attention.

"Perfect," he snickered, satisfied. The implications were deliciously favorable. Daisy being sidelined meant she was isolated, vulnerable, exactly where he wanted her.

As he absorbed the details of Daisy's medical condition, his mind began to race with possibilities. Each scenario was more sinister than the last, a twisted game of chess where he was always two moves ahead. He tapped ashes from his cigar into a crystal ashtray, a flicker of impatience crossing his features. Time was of the essence now; Daisy's temporary weakness was an opportunity he would not squander.

Rising from his chair, Lumen strode across the room to a large, ornate globe. He spun it slowly, his fingers tracing the continents until they stopped at North America. His touch drew an imaginary line from his home in Bermuda to the state of Tennessee, a wicked grin spreading across his face.

"It's time to pay a little visit," he murmured, the thrill of the hunt sparking in his eyes.

He walked back to his desk, pressed a button on his phone, and waited as the line connected.

"Prepare the jet," he instructed curtly, his voice carrying the authority and expectation of immediate obedience. "We're going to Nashville"

As he ended the call, Lumen glanced once more at the screens displaying Daisy's medical information. A dark chortle escaped him, the sound mingling with the hum of his high-tech equipment. "Rest up, Daisy," he said, affectionately. "You'll need your strength."

Chapter 13

Daisy's awareness crept back slowly, accompanied by the faint, rhythmic beeping of machines that seemed both alien and comforting. Her senses awoke in fragments: the antiseptic sting of hospital-grade disinfectant prickled her nose, overlaying the mild, almost sweet aroma of sterile linens. The distant clatter of a meal cart down the hall and the occasional squeak of rubber-soled shoes on the polished linoleum outside her door met her ears. An involuntary shiver traveled down her spine as a cool dribble from the IV needle in her arm reminded her of its presence, the fluid within feeling like ice threads weaving through her veins.

Her eyelids felt heavy as if weighed down by the gravity of her ordeal. Opening them felt like peeling back layers of darkness; the fluorescent lights above burst into her vision, too bright, too painful. Her fingers twitched slightly, the small movement barely noticeable, but enough to stir a reaction in her. As her eyes fluttered open, she tried to focus, her vision still blurry, but the sight of Jackson's silhouette leaning over her brought her a sense of comfort she hadn't realized she needed. He was watching her intently, his gaze steady and filled with concern. The faintest hint of a smile touched her lips as she registered his presence, her heart lightening just a fraction at the realization that he had been there, faithfully by her side.

She felt Jackson tighten his grip on her hand, as a rush of warmth spread up her arm. The comfort of his touch anchored her as she struggled to break through the disorientation. As she looked at him, she noticed the usual calm of his face replaced by lines of worry, his features drawn with exhaustion. But in his eyes, she caught a flicker of relief—just for a moment—as if her simple glance had reassured him she was going to be okay.

"You're in the hospital, Daisy," Jackson explained gently, leaning closer so his face came into sharper focus. "You had a pretty rough time out there, but you're safe now."

"Feels like I've been hit by a truck," Daisy said slowly, her words slurred as she fought through the fog of anesthesia and pain medication. "What's wrong with me?"

"You had surgery to stop the bleeding around your spleen and you're recovering from a concussion," Jackson explained. He gently kissed her hand. The look of worry on his face made it clear to Daisy just how serious her situation was.

"Are Roger and Riley here?" She asked as she continued to gain back her clarity.

Jackson shook his head as he smiled. "Yes, Roger is in the lobby talking on the phone with your sister, and Riley is getting a bite to eat downstairs. We haven't left since you were brought here."

Daisy's heart swelled with gratitude as she processed the words. The fact that they were there, keeping vigil over her, meant more than she could express. She'd always been independent, driven by her own goals and ambitions, but at this moment, as she lay there, she felt grateful for their support.

Her attention shifted back to Jackson. He was still in his racing pants and shirt, only his jacket removed. He hadn't changed out of his gear. It spoke volumes to Daisy about how deeply he cared for her.

"And how's Kelli doing?" she asked, her voice barely above a whisper.

Jackson offered a small, reassuring smile. "She's recuperating just one floor below us," he responded, trying to keep his tone light although his worry was palpable. "She's tough, just like you."

Daisy's mind wandered, as though she were trying to piece together a puzzle that was just out of reach. The sounds of the race—the roar of the engines, the screeching of tires, the cheers of the crowd—felt distant, almost dreamlike. A sharp pain throbbed behind her eyes, and her body still ached in places she didn't know existed. Yet beneath the haze, fragments of memories returned slowly. The blur of high speeds, her white-knuckled grip on the wheel, and the crushing weight of the crash. But there was something else. Something important, something she couldn't fully grasp yet. She blinked, trying to focus.

"I'm starting to remember what happened," Daisy mumbled, a distant look in her eyes. "You just passed me sometime after the fiftieth lap—nice maneuver, by the way," she added, managing a weak smile.

Jackson returned the smile but his expression quickly turned serious as Daisy continued.

"Tommy had been chippy with me from the start, which wasn't like him. I heard over the radio that cars behind me were starting to stall, but I didn't realize it was just Tommy and me left. I just kept going, and he was going after me fast."

She strained to recall.

"I saw the red flag and started to slow down. I heard screams over the radio, and then I felt the impact," Daisy recounted, her voice trembling. "My car flipped in the air, I hit my head, and then I think I blacked out."

Jackson listened intently and squeezed her hand.

"Jackson did Tommy... is he..." She faltered, the question hanging in the air, her voice trailing off as she struggled with the memories and half-heard snippets of conversations from her medicated haze.

Jackson's expression darkened. "Tommy didn't make it," he admitted softly, his voice thick with emotion.

Tears welled in Daisy's eyes, spilling over as she absorbed his words. "Why would he do this? Why would anyone want to hurt us like this?" Her voice cracked, each word laden with disbelief and hurt.

Jackson moved his chair closer, his free hand reaching up to gently wipe away the tears that streaked down her pale cheeks. "We're still piecing everything together," he murmured, his voice a soothing presence in the sterile chill of the hospital room.

"Agent Turner is digging into it. She believes there's more behind what Tommy did—more than we can see right now."

Daisy's breath hitched as she tried to compose herself, her mind grappling with the chaos. "It just doesn't make sense, Jackson. Tommy and I—we raced against each other for years. Why now?" Her voice was a blend of frustration and sorrow, seeking answers in a situation that seemed devoid of any logic.

"I don't know, Daisy," Jackson confessed, his voice heavy with helplessness. "I've been racking my brain, trying to make sense of it all. Tommy was... he was a lot of things, but I never thought he'd go that far."

Daisy winced as she started to rub her head. "It doesn't make sense," she murmured, her eyes searching his for answers she knew he couldn't provide.

As they sat in silence, a heaviness settled between them, loaded with unspoken questions and the harsh reality of their dangerous world. Daisy's racing career had always been filled with risks, but this betrayal cut deeper than any crash she'd ever faced on the track.

Daisy squeezed Jackson's hand, a silent thank you passing between them, her gaze lingering on his face. "I'm scared, Jackson," Daisy had never admitted fear to him before. Her bold spirit and relentless drive on and off the track defined her.

Jackson reached out and caressed her arm back and forth, "I know," he said, his voice low. "But you're not alone in this, not now, not ever." He leaned in, his presence a solid reassurance in the uncertain whirlwind of hospital monitors and whispered fears.

Daisy tilted her head as she looked at Jackson.

"I remember hearing you after the crash," Daisy suddenly recalled, her voice gaining strength.

"You were making a nuisance of yourself with the paramedics, insisting on getting in the helicopter with me."

Jackson chuckled with a smile as his eyes stayed focused on hers "Guilty as charged."

"You hate flying," Daisy said with a quiet affection.

His voice turned earnest. "You were in trouble, and I wasn't going to leave you when you needed me most."

With the smallest reserves of energy she had, Daisy placed both hands on Jackson's arm and motioned him forward until there was little space between them. Their lips met with the softest kiss. "Thank you," Daisy whispered.

The door opened quietly, and Dr. Saunders stepped into the room, her approach brisk, her expression softening as she neared Daisy's bedside. Her eyes quickly scanned the notes on her clipboard before meeting Daisy's gaze with empathy.

"Good to see you awake, Daisy," Dr. Saunders began, checking the monitors with practiced ease. "You gave us quite a scare there."

Daisy managed a weak nod, her eyes locked on the doctor, searching for reassurance. "How bad was it?"

Dr. Saunders paused. Daisy could see the doctor considering her words carefully. "Well, you sustained a significant impact, which led to internal bleeding around your spleen. We had to perform surgery to stop the bleeding and remove the damaged tissue. You also suffered a concussion, which is why your memories might feel a bit jumbled right now."

The doctor flipped through the chart on her clipboard, continuing, "Your vitals are stable now, and the surgery went smoothly, but it's crucial you rest and allow your body to heal."

Daisy's brow furrowed, absorbing the gravity of her injuries. "And the racing?" she asked, a hint of concern threading through her words.

Dr. Saunders smiled gently, understanding the importance of the question to her patient. "Let's focus on getting you through the immediate recovery first," she advised. "We can discuss your return to racing once you're further along in your recovery. It's too early to put a timeline on when you can drive again."

At that moment, Jackson squeezed Daisy's hand, offering silent support. Daisy turned to him, her expression mixed with gratitude and frustration.

Dr. Saunders added, "For now, you need plenty of rest, minimal stress, and regular check-ups. We'll be monitoring your recovery closely."

As they spoke, Roger and Riley re-entered the room. The moment their eyes landed on Daisy, their faces lit up with relief and joy. Daisy saw Riley's eyes sparkle as she stepped forward to give Daisy a gentle hug.

"We got the okay to come in from a nurse in the hallway," Roger said, smiling.

Dr. Saunders nodded, acknowledging their return. "That's fine now that she's more stable, but let's still try to keep the visits brief and calming," she instructed, her tone firm yet kind.

Daisy chuckled softly, the sound raspy but spirited. "Guess I can't kick them out just yet," she joked, eliciting a small laugh from everyone in the room.

Dr. Saunders' professional demeanor softened further with the laughter. "It's great to see you in good spirits, Daisy.

Remember, your body has been through a trauma. It's okay to take this time to heal, both physically and emotionally."

She paused, her gaze meeting Daisy's. "And you won't be able to travel for a while, certainly not back to Charlotte just yet."

Daisy absorbed the information with a nod, her mind racing through the implications. "Roger, you should go back to Charlotte to be with Morgan. Riley and I will find a place here in Nashville," she said

Jackson interrupted firmly, "No, you and Riley can stay with me."

Daisy appreciated his offer but hesitated. "Jackson, that's kind, but with the FBI involved, it could get complicated at your place."

Jackson's response was immediate and intense, his voice thick with conviction. "If you think I'm going to let anything happen to you again, then you don't know me at all." His grip tightened around her hand, his determination clear in his steely gaze.

Daisy noticed Riley's supportive smile. She could see Riley clearly was on Jackson's side, encouraging her to accept his invitation. She watched Roger nod in agreement, moved by the palpable concern Jackson displayed. Daisy looked up into Jackson's earnest eyes, feeling a surge of love that eased some of her anxiety.

"Okay," Daisy whispered, her voice soft but audible in the quiet room. Jackson leaned forward and kissed her hand.

"Alright everyone," Dr. Saunders interrupted. "I'm going to send Daisy down for some updated CT scans and I need a few moments alone with her before she goes to radiology."

Riley and Roger took turns hugging Daisy before leaving the room. Jackson lingered a few minutes longer as he kissed her cheek and tucked a blanket back in place to warm her cool arms. "I'll be right outside giving my Dad a call to let him know you're up." He said as he walked out into the hallway and closed the door.

Daisy nodded at Jackson as Dr. Saunders shined a light into Daisy's eyes, testing and evaluating the reaction of her pupils.

"Looks like you've got a great support system," Dr. Saunders commented as she widened Daisy's right eye with her thumb and pointy finger.

Daisy looked up at the wall and then back down towards her resting hands per the doctor's direction. "Yeah, they're great people. I'm lucky."

"That's good, Daisy, because there's something else I want to mention. While your physical recovery is my primary concern, we can't overlook the emotional and psychological impacts of what you've been through," Dr. Saunders intoned. "Experiencing such a traumatic event on top of what the FBI has shared with me about their investigations can have lingering effects, not just physically but mentally as well."

Daisy shifted slightly on the bed as the doctor tested her reflexes. "I appreciate that, Doctor, but I've always been pretty tough. I think I'll handle it just like I do on the track—head-on and full throttle."

Dr. Saunders nodded, acknowledging Daisy's resilience but pressing on. "It's great to have that fighting spirit, but sometimes, our minds need a bit of time to catch up with our body's healing. You might experience a range of emotions, from anxiety and fear to even something unexpected like anger or sadness. It's all normal, Daisy, but essential to address."

"Doc, I spend my days racing at over a hundred eighty miles per hour. It takes a lot to rattle me," Daisy replied as the doctor ran the eraser side of a pencil down her foot which generated a tickling sensation prompting her foot to jerk.

Dr. Saunders smiled, ready to respond to Daisy's deflection. "Yes, that's a common way of thinking from high-performance individuals like yourself used to overcoming physical pain and setbacks, but it's not just about being rattled, Daisy. Trauma can manifest in subtle ways—nightmares, flashbacks, changes in mood or behavior. Just know these are not signs of weakness but of the brain trying to process what happened."

Daisy listened to Dr. Saunders' words, her gaze fixed on the ceiling as a rush of conflicting emotions swirled within her. She had always prided herself on her ability to push through any challenge, to face adversity head-on without showing weakness. But now, lying in the hospital bed, the reality of her vulnerability hit her with unexpected force.

As Dr. Saunders continued to speak, Daisy's mind drifted back to the moment of impact, the screeching tires, the blackout. Her jaw tightened, the muscles standing out, trying to suppress the rising tide of memories threatening to overwhelm her. The thought of being trapped in that wreck sent a shiver down her spine. Deep down, Daisy knew that she was not invincible, that even the strongest armor had its weak points. Still, she attempted all she could to keep up the facade of toughness she wore like a second skin.

"I appreciate that Doc, thank you." She propped herself up for a more comfortable position on the bed.

Dr. Saunders tapped a light touch on Daisy's arm, smiling, and called for the orderlies. "Please, take Ms. Kray for her post-op imaging."

As an orderly gently wheeled Daisy into the hallway, she saw Jackson pacing by the door, on his phone. Catching her glance, he gave her a playful wink that made her think Jackson Wyatt definitely had something up his sleeve.

Chapter 14

The early morning sun bathed Jackson's ranch in a warm July glow, casting golden light across the rolling hills and valleys of the sprawling property. Horses grazed in the fields, their tails flicking gently at flies, and the soft rustle of the wind stirred the leaves of the towering trees surrounding the ranch. Birds sang from the branches, their melodies a gentle backdrop to the peacefulness that permeated the air. It was the kind of place where time seemed to slow, and the worries of the world could momentarily fade away.

Inside the ranch house, though, Daisy was restless. A week had passed since she'd left the hospital, but despite her physical recovery, her mind was far from settled. The FBI had no updates although they assured her they were "close." Every night she woke up in a cold sweat, haunted by nightmares of the crash—Tommy's car spinning out of control, the feeling of weightlessness as her car flipped through the air, and the gut-wrenching sound of metal crushing. She hadn't told anyone about the nightmares, not even Riley or Jackson, though she knew they sensed something was off. Both had given her looks of quiet concern, but Daisy brushed them off with a smile.

This morning, she'd had enough. She needed space, a chance to breathe without everyone watching her every move. More than anything, Daisy needed to feel in control again. The ranch was still quiet when she slipped out of bed, careful not to make a sound as she dressed in loose-fitting clothes that concealed her healing wounds. The FBI agents stationed around the house and at the gate were more focused on their morning routines than on her, and she used that to her advantage.

Moving quietly, she ducked out of the house and headed toward the barn. The scent of hay and leather grounded her as she stepped inside. Horses shifted in their stalls, and Chief neighed softly when he saw her. Daisy smiled and approached him, running a hand along his sleek, chestnut coat.

"Hey, boy," she whispered, her voice soft but firm. "Be gentle with me today, okay?"

Chief nudged her shoulder as if understanding. Daisy's fingers trembled slightly as she began saddling him, and a sharp twinge of discomfort reminded her of the surgery she'd just recovered from. She paused, pressing a hand to her side where the stitches had been, but shook off the feeling. She was determined.

Once Chief was saddled and bridled, Daisy grabbed a small step stool, careful not to exert too much energy as she hoisted herself onto the horse. The motion still sent a dull ache through her abdomen, but she gritted her teeth and ignored it. A duffel bag hung from the saddle horn, packed with a few essentials for when she reached her destination.

With a final glance around the barn to make sure no one was watching, Daisy clicked her tongue and urged Chief forward. The horse trotted out of the barn and into the pasture, the early morning dew still clinging to the grass. Behind her, she heard the distant shouts of the FBI agents as they realized she had left the ranch.

"Daisy!" one of them called, but she only grinned.

"Giddy up," she whispered to Chief, giving him a gentle nudge. The horse picked up speed, and Daisy let out a laugh as they galloped across the pasture, the wind whipping through her hair.

The calls of the agents faded behind her as she made her way toward the natural spring, a place on Jackson's property that she had always loved. A place where she could finally be alone.

The spring nestled in a meadow lined with wildflowers, the hills in the distance framing the scene like a painting. The water sparkled in the sunlight, cool and clear as it bubbled up from the earth. Daisy slowed Chief to a walk as they neared, her heart swelling with a mix of nostalgia and relief. This was the same spot she and Jackson had come to countless times before—before everything had gotten complicated. Dismounting Chief slowly, she tied his reins to a nearby tree and grabbed her duffel bag. The gentle rustling of leaves and the soft chirp of crickets filled the air as she spread out a large blanket near the spring. She slipped off her jacket and pants, leaving her with just a tank top and shorts, and dipped her feet into the cool water. The sensation was refreshing, prompting a calmness throughout her body.

For the first time in a week, Daisy allowed herself to relax. The warmth of the sun on her skin, the feel of the grass beneath her hands, the soothing sound of the water—it all worked to comfort her. But her thoughts, as always, returned to Jackson.

She had loved being at the ranch these past few days, even with the threat of danger looming in the background. It was Jackson who made her feel safe, not just the FBI agents or the locked gates. Every night, he stayed with her until she fell asleep, whispering soft words of comfort. He had carried her to bed when they first returned from the hospital, his arms gentle but strong. She smiled at the memory, a giddy warmth spreading through her chest.

But it was more than just the care he showed her. It was the way Jackson looked at her, the quiet intensity in his eyes that made her feel wanted, needed. It scared her a little. She wasn't used to needing anyone. She was independent, a race car driver who had fought for everything she had, including her heart.

Her mind wandered back to Daytona. The sting of betrayal still lingered, but here, at the ranch, it was harder to hold on to that pain. Her heart, her body, and her soul yearned for Jackson, but her pride, and fear, kept her guarded.

Daisy closed her eyes and let out a soft sigh, the cool water lapping at her feet as she drifted between thought and relaxation. She was just beginning to feel herself slipping into a peaceful state when she heard the sound of hooves approaching. Her head turned, and there, riding toward her on a horse, was Jackson. He slowed as he neared, his expression a mixture of concern and frustration. Pulling out his phone, he made a quick call to the FBI agents back at the ranch, assuring them that Daisy was fine and that he'd found her.

Jackson dismounted and walked over to her, his jaw tight as he approached. "Daisy, what do you think you're doing?" His voice was a low rumble. "You shouldn't be on a horse."

Daisy looked up at him, a mischievous smile playing on her lips. "Jackson, Dr. Saunders said no driving. She didn't say anything about riding a horse."

For a moment, Jackson stood there, his eyes narrowed, but then a smile tugged at the corner of his mouth, and he let out a soft laugh. "Of course, you'd find a loophole."

Daisy shrugged, her smile widening. "What can I say? I needed to get away for a bit. Clear my head."

Without another word, Jackson sat down beside her, pulling off his boots and dipping his feet into the spring next to hers. They sat in comfortable silence for a while, the only sounds were the soft bubbling of the water and the occasional rustle of leaves in the breeze. Jackson leaned back on his elbows, his body relaxed but his gaze still flickering toward Daisy.

"I know this place means a lot to you," Daisy said quietly, her voice barely louder than a whisper. "It means a lot to me, too."

Jackson turned his head to look at her, his eyes searching her face. "I'm glad you're here, Daisy. I don't think I could handle seeing you anywhere else right now."

Daisy bit her lip, her heart beating a little faster at his words. The truth of it was, she didn't want to be anywhere else either.

"By the way," Jackson said, breaking the comfortable silence with a soft chuckle, "the feds are pretty upset you didn't tell them where you were going. One of them was about ready to call in a helicopter."

Daisy grinned, with a mischievous glint in her eyes. "I overheard them saying they'd never been on horses, so I figured it was the perfect time to make my move." She laughed, brushing a loose strand of hair behind her ear. "Besides, they need to lighten up a little. I'm recovering, not imprisoned."

Jackson shook his head, though his lips curled into a smile. "And you stole my best horse, too."

Daisy raised an eyebrow, her grin widening. "I know the owner pretty well. I figured I could negotiate some leniency."

Jackson laughed heartily, the sweet sound echoing in Daisy's ears. "You've got me there."

Daisy smirked, leaning back on her hands, her fingers digging slightly into the blanket beneath her. The sun beat down on them, warming their skin, but the breeze kept the heat at bay, making the day feel like the perfect summer moment. The scent of the wildflowers and the crispness of the freshwater mingled with the earthy smell of the grass beneath them. Jackson glanced at Daisy, noticing how the sunlight caught in her hair, casting a golden hue around her.

"You know," Jackson said, his voice softer now. "I've missed seeing you like this. Relaxed. Happy."

Daisy turned her gaze to him, her smile fading into something tender, more reflective. "I've missed it, too. Being here... it's like the world slows. Like nothing else matters." Her shoulders had finally lost some of the tension they'd carried for days. She could feel herself melt into the beauty of the surroundings.

Daisy felt a pull towards Jackson even stronger in this peaceful, serene setting. She glanced at him, her heart swelling with an unfamiliar mix of emotions. "Hey," she said softly, "do you mind if I borrow your shoulder?"

Jackson turned to her, his expression softening. "It's yours," he replied, his voice warm and inviting as he laid down beside her, extending his arm out in an unspoken invitation. Daisy smiled, a gentle warmth filling her chest as she nestled into Jackson's side, resting her head against his shoulder. His arm wrapped around her, pulling her close, and he pressed a tender kiss to the top of her head, the gesture so full of care and affection that Daisy felt herself relax completely.

"Thank you," Daisy murmured after a moment, her voice quiet and sincere. "For everything. I don't know how I would've gotten through this recovery without you."

"There's nothing I wouldn't do for you," Jackson said softly. "You know that, right?"

Daisy nodded, her heart squeezing at the sincerity in his voice. She knew Jackson meant it. He had done nothing but prove it, time and time again, especially after everything that had happened. But there was still a part of her that held onto the hurt, a part she couldn't quite shake but tried her best to suppress.

She shifted in his arms, turning so that she was face-to-face with him. They lay on the blanket, under the blue sunlit sky, the world small and intimate around them. For a moment, they simply stared at each other, the connection between them deepening without the need for words. Daisy's eyes searched Jackson's, and slowly she closed the space between them.

Their lips met in a long, passionate kiss, the kind of kiss that made the world fade away. Daisy felt the intensity of it in every fiber of her being, her heart pounding in her chest as her emotions surged. Jackson responded with equal fervor, his hand cradling her cheek. When they finally broke apart, breathless and exhilarated, Jackson's voice was a rough whisper. "I love you, Daisy."

The words hit Daisy with an overwhelming wave of emotion. Tears pricked at the corners of her eyes before she could stop them. She quickly sat up, turning away from Jackson as she wiped at her eyes, her breath hitching slightly. Daisy could feel Jackson's words penetrating deep into her heart. She had never been one to easily trust or let herself be vulnerable, but here, with Jackson, it was different. Their shared history, the highs and lows they had faced together. All of it swirled inside her like a tempestuous storm. Emotions warred within her, battling for dominance over her thoughts and actions.

She knew she loved Jackson, had always loved him in a way that transcended time and distance. But there was fear too—fear of being hurt, fear of losing what they had once again.

Jackson sat up, his face lined with worry. "Daisy, what's wrong?"

She shook her head, struggling to find the words. "I've just… I've realized how much I've missed you." She took a shaky breath, tears now spilling freely. "I feel like I need you, Jackson and I'm not sure what to do with that."

Jackson smiled but stayed silent, letting her continue.

"I was so hurt after Daytona," Daisy said, her voice trembling. "That day was everything to me. My win, my father, and you… you weren't there. You were drunk with those girls." Her voice cracked, and she wrapped her arms around herself. "There's a part of me that wonders if you can truly be a part of my life. What happens when times are good for me but not for you? Can you deal with that?"

Jackson stood abruptly and paced a few steps away, placing his hands on his hips. Daisy could see he was struggling to find the right words. He looked down at her, his eyes dark with emotion.

"Daisy, I've never loved anyone as much as I love you." His voice was hoarse, filled with raw emotion. "I've been apologizing to you for months, doing everything I can to make up for what I did. When is my penance enough for you?"

Daisy looked up at him. She wanted to believe him, to trust that he could change, but the wounds of the past ran deep. "I want to believe you, Jackson. I want to trust you but…"

Jackson interrupted Daisy before she could continue. His words burst forth like a thunderstorm, each one crashing against the walls around Daisy's heart.

"I'm human, Daisy!" Jackson said, his voice rising. "I made a mistake—one I regret more than anything. I've been here. I've done everything I can to prove to you that I love you, that I'm here for you. But you have to let go of the past. You have to let me in. Let me care for you. Let me love you."

Tension crackled between them, and the sound of approaching hooves broke the tension in the air. Papa Joe and one of the ranch's wranglers appeared over the hill, their horses trotting toward the spring.

Jackson saw them and turned back to Daisy, his face hardening. He grabbed his boots and quickly slid them back on his feet.

"You can ride back with them," he said quietly, motioning toward his father and Randy, one of his trusted ranch wranglers. Without waiting for a reply, he turned and began saddling his horse.

Daisy sat in silence as she tried to process the intensity of her conflicting emotions while at the same time not wanting to say anything else to hurt Jackson.

As she watched Jackson mount his horse, Papa Joe rode up beside him, the elder Wyatt's eyes narrowing. Daisy could overhear their exchange.

"What's wrong, son?"

"Damned Daytona, Dad. Damned Daytona." With that, Jackson dug his heels into his horse's sides and galloped away.

Daisy watched Jackson go as she overheard Papa Joe talking to Randy. "Head back to the ranch, Randy," he instructed. "I'll stay with Daisy."

Randy departed, leaving Papa Joe alone with Daisy near the windswept hills. As he dismounted his horse and approached her, he exuded a calm and understanding presence, like a weathered oak tree standing strong against the storms of life. He said nothing for a moment, just watched her with the quiet wisdom of a man who had seen the world and knew its troubles. As he sat down on the blanket beside her, he reached out, pulling her into a warm embrace. Daisy leaned into him, feeling herself melting into his steady and comforting strength, releasing the tears that she had been holding back.

"You want to tell me what happened?" Papa Joe asked gently, his voice soft and fatherly.

Daisy took a deep breath, wiping at her eyes. "I don't know," she whispered. "It's just… everything. I'm scared of a lot of things right now, including falling for your son again."

Papa Joe nodded slowly in understanding as he carefully stood up from the ground and reached his hand out to Daisy. "Let's take a walk."

Daisy took his hand as she looked at him in curiosity. Papa Joe walked beside Daisy, the sound of their footsteps mingling with the soft rustle of the wildflowers in the breeze. For a while, neither of them spoke, the peacefulness of the surroundings offering a quiet reprieve. As they neared the horses, Papa Joe paused, glancing at Daisy with a thoughtful expression.

"You know Jackson was miserable without you. I'd never seen him so lost." Papa Joe offered as he skipped a stone onto the spring.

Daisy glanced up at him. "He was lost?"

Papa Joe smirked "Oh yes. Like a sad-lookin' puppy dog. And boy was he fit to be tied when he saw that pro quarterback Brock Myers at that charity auction get the winning bid to have dinner with you! Land sakes he was a bear to live with for weeks."

Daisy couldn't help but let out a small chuckle at the image of Jackson being jealous over something as trivial as a charity auction. Papa Joe's storytelling had a way of weaving a comforting blanket around her, making her feel at ease even in the midst of her inner turmoil.

"He was jealous of Brock Myers?" Daisy raised an eyebrow, genuinely surprised.

Papa Joe nodded, his eyes twinkling with amusement. "Oh, you have no idea, darlin'. He was ready to challenge that quarterback to a race just to prove himself."

Daisy appreciated the way Papa Joe shared these details with her, making her see a different side of Jackson, one that tugged at her heartstrings. Then his voice took a more serious tone as he changed the subject to racing.

"Daisy," he said, his voice soft but steady, "do you realize you're a better driver than Jackson?"

Daisy blinked, taken aback by the bluntness of the question. She stopped walking, her brow furrowing slightly. "What are you talking about?"

Papa Joe turned to face her fully, leaning against his horse's saddle as he studied her. "You heard me. You're a better driver than him. Always have been."

Daisy shook her head, an uncomfortable laugh escaping her lips. "I don't know about that, Papa Joe. Jackson's one of the best."

"He's good," Papa Joe agreed, nodding slowly. "But you're better. And deep down, I think you've always known that." He paused. "But more importantly, Jackson knows it."

Daisy looked away, her gaze drifting toward the rolling hills in the distance. "I don't know if that's true," she muttered, kicking at a loose stone on the ground. "And even if it is, why does it matter?"

Papa Joe's eyes softened as he took a step closer to her. "It matters because falling in love's hard enough. But falling in love with someone who you know is better than you at the one thing you've devoted your life to and who happens to be your fiercest competitor every Sunday?" He whistled low. "That's a whole other kind of challenge."

Daisy glanced up at him, her confusion evident. "But that shouldn't affect him... should it?"

Papa Joe let out a deep sigh, rubbing his chin. "It shouldn't, no. But Jackson's competitive, just like you. And while he loves you, he's also had to reckon with the fact that the woman he's fallen so deeply for is the one who outshines him on the racetrack. That can mess with a man's head, and make him question things. And still, despite that, he wants you. He needs you."

Daisy frowned, the complexity of the situation beginning to sink in. "You think that's why he got so messed up at Daytona?"

Papa Joe nodded slowly. "Part of it. He's had to learn to deal with a lot—his love for you, his pride as a driver, your father's legacy, and his insecurities. That day, when he saw you win after his debacle with the fuel line... it wasn't just about the race. It was about his fear of losing you, feeling like he wasn't enough for you."

Daisy felt a pang in her chest, a mixture of sympathy and sadness. "I never thought of it that way... I never thought Jackson felt that way."

Papa Joe smiled gently, resting a hand on her shoulder. "He wouldn't want you to know. Jackson's proud, maybe too proud. But he loves you more than anything, Daisy. He's just had to wrestle with his demons on top of trying to be the man you deserve."

"So what do I do?" Daisy asked quietly, her voice barely above a whisper.

Papa Joe squeezed her shoulder gently. "Well Daisy, if this were a race, you'd be driving under caution; maintaining your position until the hazards are clear, but it's impossible to live life like that. You can't keep one foot out the door forever. He's been trying to prove to you that he's worthy of your love. But maybe what he needs is for you to show him that he doesn't have to prove anything."

Daisy swallowed hard, the truth of his words settling deep within her. She glanced up at Papa Joe, her eyes softening with gratitude.

"You're a good man, Papa Joe," she said, her voice thick with emotion.

Papa Joe chuckled, pulling her into a brief hug. "Just a man who's seen a lot, sweetheart. I want the best for both of you. Jackson's got a lot of fight in him, but he's not fighting against you—he's fighting for you."

Daisy leaned into the embrace for a moment before pulling back and giving him a nod. "Thank you."

As Daisy processed Papa Joe's words, myriad emotions churned within her. She couldn't deny the truth in his insights, the layers of complexity that had colored her relationship with Jackson. Her heart ached with newfound understanding, a blend of sympathy and remorse for not seeing things from his perspective sooner.

As he started to get the horses ready for the journey back to the ranch, Papa Joe's smile widened just a little too much, a glint in his eye like he was holding something back. Daisy noticed it immediately, the way his lips curled with mischief and his eyes sparkled as if he had a secret. There was something more to his expression, something unsaid that he was toying with.

Daisy raised an eyebrow, her curiosity piqued. "What's with that smile on your face? What aren't you telling me?"

Papa Joe paused, letting out a soft sigh as he seemed to consider something, clearly amused by whatever thought had crossed his mind. Then he looked at Daisy, his grin slipping into something more playful. "Well, Jackson might not like this, but I think now is the perfect time."

Daisy's confusion deepened. "What do you mean?"

Papa Joe chuckled, his voice full of excitement. "There's something I need to show you."

Chapter 15

In the industrial stillness of a remote warehouse outside of Nashville, Lumen Ross paced slowly in his command center. Monitors lined the walls, displaying endless streams of code and data. Custom-built servers hummed softly, their lights flickering in sync with the rhythm of his steps. On a central workstation, an array of advanced control panels and holographic screens lay in front of him, ready to execute his commands. A pair of pristine sports cars sat parked in the corner, their engines silent but poised.

Lumen paused in front of one of the screens, watching the security footage he intercepted from the cameras at Jackson Wyatt's ranch. There she was—Daisy—sneaking out of the house, her movements graceful even as she evaded the watchful eyes of her FBI detail. His lip curled in disgust at the sight of Jackson rushing to saddle up his horse to find Daisy.

"Always the cowboy aren't you Jackson?"

Taking a deep breath, Lumen forced himself to step away from the monitor. He needed control, precision. He couldn't let his temper cloud his judgment, not now. Not when he was so close. He paced toward the corner of the warehouse, where a sleek, red sports car gleamed under the fluorescent lights. Each curve and angle was meticulously crafted to evoke a sense of power and speed.

"My dear," he whispered, his voice a hushed murmur that reverberated through the empty warehouse. "You are a masterpiece. A symphony of engineering and artistry. They may call you a car, but you are so much more than that. You are a marvel, a testament to human ingenuity and passion."

Lumen's hand ran delicately over the smooth surface of the vehicle, his fingertips tracing the contours as if seeking some hidden message within its sleek frame. He had poured his heart and soul into this machine, infusing it with everything he was—ambition, determination, and a touch of madness. It was more than a car to him; it was a symbol of his power and control.

"Your curves are perfection," he whispered, his eyes gleaming with a dangerous intensity.

With a gentle touch against the handle, the wing doors opened up on each side as if preparing for flight.

The vessel's interior was designed with both luxury and cutting-edge technology in mind. The cockpit was enveloped in smooth, black leather, and the seats contoured perfectly to the shape of a body, providing comfort even at high speeds. The leather had a soft, buttery texture under the fingertips, but it was durable—resilient to the wear and tear of the powerful forces the car was capable of exerting. Ambient lighting ran along the edges of the interior, casting a soft blue glow inside.

There was no traditional steering wheel, no gear shift, and no pedals. In their place was a wide, curved digital console that extended across the entire dashboard. The display was a sleek touch-sensitive screen, seamlessly integrated into the car's design. It was activated by touch, voice command, or even gesture control. Lumen could bring up detailed maps, camera feeds, real-time diagnostics and advanced AI interfaces with a flick of his fingers, all on the massive, glassy dashboard that spanned in front of him.

The car was completely autonomous. A hidden array of sensors, cameras, and complex systems allowed it to navigate any terrain with pinpoint precision, making it more aware of its surroundings than any human driver ever could be. The AI was not only sophisticated—it was ruthless in its efficiency. Lumen had personally overseen the development of the car's operating system, ensuring it was programmed for speed, evasion, and, when necessary, pursuit.

In the center console, where an armrest might normally be, there was a retractable control panel. Lumen could bring it up with the press of a button, revealing a complex set of holographic displays that hovered in mid-air. These projected screens allowed Lumen to override the car's autonomous functions if he chose, offering full manual control through a joystick-like mechanism that rose from the console. But he rarely used it. He preferred to be in control without needing to touch the wheel.

The windshield was another marvel of technology—a wide, high-definition augmented reality display that showed everything from maps to incoming threat assessments. It wasn't just a view of the road; it was an interactive screen that fed Lumen information about his surroundings. Red lines would trace potential dangers, green paths would highlight the safest routes and a constant feed of data streamed across the bottom, detailing weather conditions, vehicle diagnostics, and surveillance feeds from external cameras.

The sound system, designed to deliver pristine audio, was integrated into every surface of the car. It could cancel out exterior noise entirely, creating a bubble of silence if Lumen needed to focus. Or, with a command, it could pipe in the steady hum of the car's engine and the sound of the road—whichever suited his mood.

In addition to its technological prowess, the car exuded opulence. A small compartment near the passenger seat discreetly housed a humidor, keeping Lumen's cigars perfectly fresh. Every detail of the car was crafted with the dual purpose of control and indulgence.

As Lumen sat in the cockpit, he acknowledged that this was more than just a car. It was his mobile fortress, a self-driving extension of his will. From here, he could monitor his plans, control his network, and make split-second decisions with the efficiency of a machine but the mind of a man who thrived on chaos.

This car was a symbol of everything Lumen had become—technologically superior, relentlessly intelligent, and always one step ahead of those who dared to cross him.

Returning to his desk, Lumen picked up a cigar, lighting it with a practiced flick of his wrist. The thick smoke curled around him. He took a slow drag, the bitter taste of the tobacco filling his lungs as his mind sharpened.

The time to enact his revenge was near. Everything was under his control. He had the technology, the connections, the wealth. And soon, he would have the satisfaction of watching Daisy crumble beneath the pressure of his plans.

His phone buzzed, interrupting his contemplation. He glanced down at the screen, a smirk tugging at his lips. It was another update from his insider at the ranch, someone feeding him detailed reports of Daisy's every move.

"Daisy evaded the FBI again. She's restless and emotionally fragile."

Lumen's smirk widened. Of course, she was fragile. That was the plan. The nightmares, the trauma—he knew how to push people to the edge, to make them doubt everything they thought they knew. And Daisy was already teetering. She had no idea that Lumen saw her life as a puppet show where he was the one pulling the strings.

He took another drag from his cigar, the smoke curling lazily into the air. He fast-forwarded through the footage to see Daisy returning to the ranch with Jackson's father.

"Enjoy your moments of peace with the old man, Daisy." Lumen snuffed out his cigar, grinding the ashes into a nearby tray.

He walked over to his computer and tapped a few keys on his laptop, bringing up a new screen—an encrypted message with the official FBI seal.

"Now let me get to work on getting the FBI out of my way."

Chapter 16

The garage on Jackson Wyatt's ranch was spacious and orderly, the air thick with the scent of oil, rubber, and old leather. Tools hung meticulously from the walls, and various car parts, engines, and gadgets were scattered around, each in its designated spot. Along the far side, Jackson's collection of both classic and new sports cars gleamed under the soft, golden light from the late afternoon sun. Some were polished to perfection, while others were in various stages of restoration. Yet none of the sights held Daisy's attention quite like the car parked in front of her.

A 1967 Mustang GT500, with its original Wimbledon white paint and blue stripes, gleamed under the fluorescent lights. Daisy stood frozen in disbelief, her hand still lightly resting on the driver's door handle as if she were afraid to touch it any further, worried it might disappear like a dream. The car was a piece of her past—a symbol of a time long gone. And yet, here it was, returned to her after so many years.

Riley knelt by the front of the Mustang, examining it with the sharp eye of a mechanic, her hands brushing over the pristine chrome bumper.

"Tell me again how Jackson managed to find this?" Riley asked. The rarest of smiles tugged at the corner of her lips as she inspected the classic muscle car's spotless condition.

Daisy blinked, snapping out of her daze.

"Papa Joe told me," she began, her voice soft as she stared at the car. "While I was in the hospital, Jackson called Papa Joe and asked if he could track down the VIN of the Mustang. It's the same car I used to own when Jackson and I first met." She ran her fingers along the cool metal, a wave of nostalgia flooding through her.

"It was sold at a charity auction a year before Dad died. I always regretted donating it, but it was for a good cause."

Riley stood, wiping her hands on her jeans as she moved closer to Daisy. "And Papa Joe tracked it down?"

"Yeah," Daisy said, nodding slowly. "When the nurse took me down for more tests after I saw the doctor in the hospital, I caught a glimpse of Jackson in the hall on the phone and he gave me this playful smile like he was up to something. Apparently, he was talking to Papa Joe asking him the get the wheels in motion to try and get my

Mustang back. Morgan was in on it as well. The auction house still had the buyer's information. The guy wasn't willing to let it go without a fight, but Jackson..." She trailed off, smiling slightly. "He told Papa Joe to pay whatever it cost, no matter the price. He said he knew the car would bring me joy when I needed it the most."

Riley raised an eyebrow. "That's some dedication. And judging by the looks of this beauty, it was worth every penny." She gave the car an appreciative pat before turning back to Daisy. "So, does this help? Clear your head a bit about Jackson?"

Daisy exhaled, her breath shaky. "It's more than that," she admitted. "It's the fact that he remembered. Not just the car, but that moment. The day we met... my dad's garage, me working under the hood. I was so focused, and he came in like this big shot racer."

She smiled at the memory, her eyes misting over. "I didn't even look at him, but I guess he remembered everything about that day."

Riley leaned against the hood, crossing her arms. "Seems to me that Jackson's been thinking about you and your happiness for a long time, even when things got rocky."

Daisy nodded slowly, her voice soft as she spoke again. "Even with everything going on—this... danger, this uncertainty—I can see a path forward with him. I love him, Riley. Despite all the pain, despite Daytona... I still love him."

Riley smirked. "Took you long enough to admit that." She gave Daisy a playful nudge with her elbow. "But hey, better late than never. You talk to Morgan about all this?"

Daisy laughed, rolling her eyes. "Yes. And she joked that her husband of eight years has never done anything like that for her."

Riley snorted, shaking her head. "Sounds like Morgan!"

"But she also reminded me of how much Jackson's done over the past five months to make up for his screw-up at Daytona," Daisy continued, her voice growing more thoughtful. "He never left my side in the hospital. Every night, he was there."

Riley walked around the car, crouching again to inspect the tires. "And he's still here. I mean, come on, Daisy—this car isn't just a gesture. This is him showing you that he's all in, no matter what happened in the past." She glanced up, her eyes sharp with understanding. "You gonna tell him?"

Daisy sighed, running her hand through her hair as she leaned back against the garage wall.

"He's doing a photo shoot near the loft barn for a sponsor. Since racing is still shut down because of the FBI investigation, all the drivers have clearance to do is business and sponsorship stuff that isn't public-facing."

Riley grinned at Daisy, pushing herself up to her feet and wiping her hands on a rag. "Well, everything looks good and as you left it except for the new gear shift the last owner installed but it's a nice upgrade. Very smooth."

Daisy took note, shaking her head as Riley closed the car door and made her way to the front of the garage.

"I'm gonna leave you alone to catch up with your car, Daisy. And don't try to slip away again—your FBI detail's right outside the door, probably sweating bullets."

"Yeah, I hear they brought someone in who can ride a horse this time." Daisy joked. She heard Riley's laugh echo through the garage as she made her way out.

"Good luck with that," Riley teased, giving Daisy one last glance. "Just remember—sometimes people do things that surprise you in the best way possible. Jackson's trying to be that person for you. Don't make it harder than it needs to be."

Daisy cocked her head and nodded at Riley in understanding. Daisy then turned back to walk toward the car, her heart still racing. The garage was quiet now, save for the distant rustle of the breeze outside. She touched the steering wheel, the smooth, worn leather cool beneath her palm. The car aged, but it was still as powerful as ever, a reminder of who she used to be before life had gotten so complicated. Before the FBI, the threats, and the danger looming over her every move.

She slid into the driver's seat, resting her hands on the wheel, and closed her eyes. Memories flooded over her— the sound of her dad's voice as he coached her through repairs and the way Jackson had watched her that day, admiring her confidence and skill.

A tear slipped down her cheek before she wiped it away quickly. Jackson had done all of this for her. He'd brought back a piece of her life that she thought was gone forever. And that gesture, more than any apology or word he could have said, proved to her how much he loved her. Despite everything, despite her doubts and the lingering hurt from Daytona, she knew deep down that she loved him too.

Daisy stepped out of the garage, the Nashville air caressing her skin, heavy with the scent of warmed hay and blooming wildflowers. The twilight sky stretched wide and soft above the ranch, painted in hues of gold and violet as the evening settled in. Her heart raced with anticipation as her eyes scanned the path ahead, knowing she needed to see Jackson.

She spotted him, standing at the fence across from the loft barn, a cozy refuge at the ranch for overflow guests with country charm and all the comforts of home.

Jackson dressed head to toe in black—a sleek contrast to the rustic backdrop of the ranch. His charcoal slacks fit him perfectly, emphasizing the strength of his legs. His shirt, also midnight shaded, was only half-buttoned, and the sight of him stirred something deep inside Daisy, a pull she couldn't resist. He was dangerously alluring.

Her body reacted instinctively, a warmth unfurling low in her stomach as she watched him. There was something about Jackson in that moment—his confidence, his presence—that made her pulse quicken, her attraction to him undeniable. She had always found him attractive, but with the twilight draped around him, and the air thick with the scent of the earth, she found him irresistible.

Jackson said goodbye to the crew from the photo shoot, his voice low and steady. The way he leaned casually against the fence sent a fresh wave of attraction through her. Daisy summoned the courage to approach him.

As if sensing her presence, he turned, his eyes catching hers. For a brief moment, something flickered across his face—surprise, followed by warmth, and something more that Daisy could feel down to her core.

"Hello Ms. Kray, this is a welcomed surprise," he called out, his smile broadening as she made her way towards him.

Daisy smiled, her heart thumping in her chest as she reached out to embrace him. She closed her eyes savoring the feeling of his grip around her.

"Daisy, what is it?" he asked tenderly.

She gently loosened herself from Jackson and looked him into his eyes as she wrapped her arms behind his neck. "You found my car. My GT500."

Jackson glanced at the ground as he kept his hands on Daisy's hips. Her eyes searched his face for a response.

"Yes, Daisy, I found it," Jackson admitted, meeting her gaze with an intensity that conveyed his sincerity. "But tell me, how did *you* find it?"

Daisy crossed her arms over her chest, a soft smile playing on her lips. "After you left the meadow this morning,

Papa Joe took me to the garage today. He thought now was the right time to show me."

Jackson looked caught off guard as he processed what she said. His lips parted as if he was about to speak, but then he shook his head, a chuckle escaping him. His voice was warm, but there was a hint of self-deprecation as he smiled. "My dad always had good timing."

"He does," Daisy agreed, her gaze soft as she stepped even closer, the faint scent of leather and cedarwood drifting from Jackson. "It was perfect, Jackson. It's one of the nicest things anyone has ever done for me."

Jackson's expression softened, a rare vulnerability crossing his features. "How could I forget that car?" His voice dipped, filled with emotion. "It reminds me of the moment I first met you. You were working on the engine under the hood. Your hair was pulled back and you had on a green Kray Motorsports t-shirt and oil-spotted jeans."

Daisy stood shocked that Jackson remembered the details of their first meeting so long ago. She tilted her head to the side as Jackson gently wiped away a tear falling down her cheek as he continued.

"I also know how special it was because your dad gave it to you," Jackson declared as he played with strands of Daisy's hair between his fingertips.

Daisy's heart swelled at his words. Hearing Jackson remember something so meaningful from their past, especially connected to her father, made her feel overwhelmed with affection. The Mustang wasn't just a car—it was a piece of her history, a bridge to the person she was before everything changed. And Jackson knew that. He understood its importance, just like he had grown to understand her. She remained speechless taking in the moment.

Jackson's brow wrinkled slightly. "Daisy, about earlier… I shouldn't have lost it like that in the meadow. I—"

Before he could finish, Daisy lifted her fingers to his lips, silencing him. Her touch was gentle, soft, and her eyes met his with understanding. "You don't have to apologize," she whispered, her voice carrying all the warmth and tenderness she felt for him at that moment.

The feel of her fingers against his lips sent a current of electricity down her spine, and for a moment, everything seemed to still around them. The evening air buzzed with energy, the scent of the earth strong, the distant songs of crickets blending into the background.

Their eyes locked, and before she could think twice, Daisy rose on her toes and pressed her lips to his, slow and tender. The kiss deepened almost immediately, a fire sparking between them as she felt Jackson's hands slide down her back, pulling her closer, his mouth moving against hers with a fierce, controlled hunger. The feel of his stubble against her soft skin, the warmth of his lips, the way his strong hands held her as if he never wanted to let go—everything about Jackson in that moment made her ache for him.

Daisy broke the kiss, breathless, her eyes searching his. "I love you," she whispered, the words spilling from her lips before she could stop them. "I've been scared to admit it, scared to even think about it after everything, but it's the truth. You make me feel like I'm the only thing that matters in the world."

Without a word, Jackson wrapped his arms around her waist, pulling her into him. Daisy let out a small gasp as their bodies connected, her hands resting against his chest, feeling the steady thrum of his heartbeat beneath her palm. The warmth of his skin against her fingers, the rough texture of his half-unbuttoned shirt, and the scent of him—earthy and masculine—made her dizzy with longing.

She leaned into his neck, kissing the nape and brushing her face against his as she whispered into his ear. "I need you, Jackson."

And in that moment, there was no uncertainty, no doubt. Jackson scooped her up into his arms effortlessly, the strength in his hold making her feel weightless as he carried her toward the barn loft, which was bathed in the warm glow of string lights. The wooden beams above reached across the ceiling like protective arms, cradling the space in a cozy embrace.

As Jackson carried Daisy up the creaking staircase to the loft, her heart raced with anticipation, her body trembling with desire.

Jackson gently laid Daisy down on the bed in the center of the loft. The pillows, plump and inviting, were covered in soft linen cases adorned with lace trim that framed the edges elegantly. They beckoned Daisy to sink into their embrace, promising comfort and solace in their fluffy depths. Jackson set himself beside her, his hand caressing her face as his eyes looked at her with concern.

"Daisy, are you sure you're okay to…I mean, your surgery and…" His voice was gentle, his touch careful as if he were afraid to break her.

Daisy smiled softly, reaching up to kiss the curve of his neck, her lips grazing his skin. His presence hypnotic and soothing.

"As long as you let me drive," she whispered playfully, her fingers already working at the buttons of his shirt.

"Absolutely." Jackson declared. He then nudged his lips to the lobe of her ear and whispered in a low, husky voice, "Drive me."

Daisy's fingers glided over the firm, chiseled terrain of Jackson's chest, feeling each ridge and valley of muscle beneath her touch. His hands wandered over her figure with an insatiable curiosity, leaving a trail of goosebumps in their wake as he explored every inch of her with a reverence bordering on worship. Electricity sparked from his fingertips like a live wire, sending jolts of pleasure coursing through her veins with each caress. She pressed closer to him with mounting urgency, trying to satiate a thirst that only seemed to grow stronger with every second.

She could feel his breath against her skin like a warm breeze as his lips traced a path along her neck. He moved up to her ear where he whispered, "I can't get enough of you." An overwhelming tide of emotions swept over her heart—an intoxicating mixture of love and lust that threatened to drown her in its intensity.

His eyes locked onto hers with an almost primal fervor. She didn't dare look away, compelled by the wildfire burning within his gaze and wanting him to see her matching passion.

Their bodies moved together as if guided by some unseen force, old as time and as inevitable as the ebb and flow of the tide: a dance that was both familiar yet ever-changing in its complexity and beauty. She marveled at how perfectly their bodies fit together like pieces of an intricate puzzle, crafted by fate for each other. In Jackson's embrace, she felt accepted and cherished, which gave her the courage to expose her heart in its rawest form.

She found herself captivated by him, unable to escape even if she wanted to—not that she had any desire to; she craved this moment of blissful harmony and sensory overload as much as he did. Caught up in their entwined bodies and whispered confessions of adoration, she barely noticed time slipping away as they became lost in their own little world. Anything outside faded into nothingness as they cocooned themselves in their private haven where nothing could encroach upon their sanctuary—concern, worry, insecurity, all were washed away by the tender pleasures that enveloped them.

Yet, amidst the wonderment of their evening, the pervading darkness outside was no longer just the cover of night, but a harbinger of impending danger, its presence underscored by the distant, eerie cry of a coyote—a sound that pierced the stillness, a reminder of the threats lurking just beyond.

Chapter 17

Maps and charts detailing various ongoing investigations covered the walls of Agent Turner's FBI office. Piles of case files sat neatly stacked beside a state-of-the-art computer system that hummed softly in the background. Neatly tucked beside the case files, were small brass plaques engraved with the FBI seal—a constant reminder of her dedication to the law and her unwavering commitment to playing by the book.

Agent Turner glanced at the clock. She sat restless in her chair waiting for a debrief from FBI Cyber Special Agent Ethan Fields. The young agent had an uncanny ability to make sense of the chaotic digital landscape she struggled to grasp.

A knock rapped at her door.

"Come in," she called out.

Agent Ethan Fields entered the office with anxious energy, balancing a laptop under one arm and a stack of files clutched in the other. He was exactly what most expect from a cyber agent in his mid-twenties: geeky, slightly awkward, with glasses that always slid halfway down his nose. Although the late forty-something Agent Turner often clashed with the younger Agent Fields, she couldn't deny his exceptional technical knowledge and appreciated his respect for her tenure at the bureau.

"Agent Turner." Fields cleared his throat nervously as he placed his files and laptop on her desk and sat down, his lanky frame barely filling the chair. "Uh, thanks for seeing me. I've got the latest from the cyber team. You're going to want to hear this."

"Great." Agent Turner crossed her arms. "What did you find out?"

Fields shuffled through his files and opened his laptop. Turner had to stifle a smile—he was bright but green. Still, despite his awkwardness, she could sense the importance of what he was about to reveal.

Fields cleared his throat again, glancing at his computer screen before launching into his findings.

"We've confirmed that the cars in the Tennessee 400 were compromised by a targeted cyberattack. Specifically, it was an AI-generated malware that infiltrated their telemetry systems."

Agent Turner raised an eyebrow, folding her arms. "Telemetry systems? You're already losing me, Fields. Start from the beginning—like you're explaining this to a third grader."

"Right, uh… third-grade level," Fields muttered, flustered. "Okay, think of the race cars like really advanced remote-controlled cars, okay? Each car's computer sends information back to the pit crew over a wireless network. Kinda like how walkie-talkies work."

Turner leaned back slightly, her eyes softening as she caught onto his analogy. "Alright. Go on."

Fields' voice gained confidence. "Someone hacked into that network. Imagine if a hacker intercepted those walkie-talkie signals and pretended to be the pit crew. They could give the car all kinds of fake commands—telling it to stall, for example, even though the crew never said to."

Agent Turner's eyes narrowed further, her fingers uncrossing and resting on the desk, a sign she was now fully invested.

"So they hijacked the cars' systems remotely?"

"Exactly," Fields said, more animated now. "But it's even smarter than that. The malware—this virus—was AI-generated. It wasn't just a basic virus. It learned from the system it infected.

Agent Turner raised a skeptical eyebrow, her arms unfolding as she leaned in. "Explain that to me in a way I can visualize."

Fields nodded quickly, warming to the explanation. "Okay, imagine this. All the cars are tuned into the wrong radio station, right? The malware made sure that when they 'listened' for the crew's instructions, they got the wrong message. So, instead of hearing 'keep going,' they heard 'shut down.' That's why they all stalled at the same time."

Agent Turner's expression softened, showing she was following along. "So, it's like someone switched all the radios to a fake frequency."

"Exactly," Fields said, pleased with her interpretation. "And here's the kicker—the malware wasn't just pre-programmed to do one thing. It was AI-generated, which means it learned and adapted from the system it infected. Once inside the car's telemetry systems, it understood the flow of data and adjusted itself to deliver the most effective commands. It's like a virus with a brain."

Agent Turner pondered the information, her fingers drumming lightly on her desk. "How did the cars get hacked with this virus?"

Fields leaned forward in his chair, his eyes wide with excitement. His hands moved animatedly as he explained, his voice full of energy. "The virus infiltrated the cars' communication systems during a routine software update before the race." He couldn't help but pause for a moment, letting the significance sink in before continuing. His hands were practically dancing in the air as he elaborated. "Then, when the hacker sent a command during the race, the virus told the cars to cut off their engines. The cars received the fake commands at the same moment, which is why it looked like a mass mechanical failure."

Agent Turner leaned back, her arms crossing again. "And once the damage was done, the virus wiped itself?"

"Yep," Fields replied, now fully in his element. "It's like a magician who pulls off a trick and vanishes before you can figure out how. The virus erased its digital footprint, leaving almost no trace. Almost."

Agent Turner leaned forward, elbows on her desk now, focus laser sharp. "*Almost?*"

Fields hesitated. "The virus was designed to be invisible, but we did find a clue—something small, but important." He pulled out a folder and pushed it toward her.

"The code structure of this virus… it's eerily similar to the one used to hack Daisy Kray's medical records."

Agent Turner's fingers tightened around the edge of the folder, a ripple of adrenaline flooding her system. *This is it,* she thought. *We might finally be closing in on a potential perpetrator.*

Fields continued. "We traced the code structures to an overseas tech company. They've been accused of creating malicious software using AI. And here's the kicker—one of their silent investors? A former race car driver named Lumen Ross."

Agent Turner's face darkened at the name. "Lumen Ross?"

Fields nodded. "Yeah. The guy had a history of causing trouble, both on and off the track. He was even banned from racing. What makes this interesting is his background in AI and technology. He has made a fortune investing in companies that develop cutting-edge software, including AI-generated tools—tools that could easily be adapted for something like this."

Agent Turner sat up, her mind racing. "So, Ross isn't just an ex-driver. He's got the technical know-how and the resources to pull something like this off?"

"For sure," Ethan said. "We don't have direct proof but the fact that a former race car driver with a grudge against the industry is connected to a company using malicious AI? Plus, in looking at Tommy Crow's cell phone records he made and received calls from anonymous numbers we've been able to geo-target to locations where Lumen Ross has homes."

Agent Turner took a closer look at the report. "Says here Ross is a bit of a nomad."

"Yeah, he's slippery," Fields confirmed. "Multiple properties all over the world, shell companies, and connections to a lot of shady characters. If he's behind this, he's covering his tracks well."

Agent Turner set the file down, her jaw tightening. "Good work, Fields. I'll dig into this Ross angle. We need to see if there's anything else tying him directly to the malware or Daisy."

Fields smiled, clearly relieved at the praise. "Thanks, Agent Turner. I'll keep working on the tech side. Let me know if you need anything."

"Will do," Agent Turner said, watching as Fields gathered his things. Before he left, she added, "Don't be a stranger. We're going to crack this thing, and I might need your help again."

Fields grinned awkwardly and nodded. "Anytime."

Once he left, Agent Turner searched "Lumen Ross" in the FBI database. There had to be more to Ross' connection to this whole thing, and she wasn't going to stop until she figured it out.

Chapter 18

The late afternoon breeze stirred the air, drifting through the large kitchen windows of Jackson Wyatt's ranch, gently rustling the curtains and casting a soft, serene ambiance over the rustic wooden table where Daisy Kray and Agent Turner sat.

Jackson's in-home cook had just served them coffee, leaving steaming mugs in front of them. Daisy sat with her hands wrapped around her cup, the warmth of it comforting, though she couldn't shake the tension that clung to her ever since Agent Turner arrived.

The no-nonsense professional took a long sip, her sharp eyes scanning Daisy with a mixture of curiosity and amusement. "You know, you're looking surprisingly good, considering everything you've been through."

Daisy smiled, her cheeks flushing slightly. "Thanks. I've been getting plenty of rest out here. Jackson's ranch has been a nice escape if I'm honest."

Agent Turner raised an eyebrow and smirked, her tone teasing as she responded. "Rest? From what my agents have been telling me, you seem to be pretty active. Getting around quite well."

Daisy blushed deeper, sensing the playful undertone. "What exactly are you implying?" she asked, a girlish grin spreading across her face.

Agent Turner leaned back in her chair, her smirk widening. "Well, word around here is that 'Jaisy' might be back together."

Daisy cocked her head, clearly caught off guard. "Wait—how do you even know about Jaisy? I thought you weren't into racing."

Agent Turner chuckled softly, setting her mug down. "I'm not, but Jackson filled me in on a few things. He told me how the media used that nickname when you two were a thing. Guess it was a big deal back then."

Daisy's lips twitched into a smile, memories of the media frenzy and their whirlwind romance flashing through her mind. "So… what else did he tell you?" she asked curiously.

Agent Turner raised a hand, shaking her head with mock seriousness. "Sorry, Daisy. That's classified. But I will say—he's a good egg. From what I've seen, he genuinely cares about you."

Daisy's smile softened as she lowered her gaze, her heart fluttering at the thought of Jackson's loyalty. She was quiet for a moment, letting Agent Turner's words settle.

Agent Turner shifted in her chair, taking another sip of her coffee. "How's Kelli Foster doing?" she asked, breaking the silence.

Daisy sighed softly. "She's out of the hospital now, staying with her parents nearby. As you know the FBI detail is also with her. She's recovering, but it's slow. She can't travel yet."

Turner nodded thoughtfully. "What about your sister Morgan?"

Daisy's face softened. "Morgan's doing okay. Very pregnant and trying to get rest. But she's worried, you know. I've tried to reassure her, but it's hard. I'm just glad Roger's with her—he's been great at keeping her calm."

Agent Turner's gaze flicked toward the windows, where extra FBI agents were posted around the property. She turned back to Daisy, her expression serious. "Speaking of protection, I've brought a few more agents today. Just precautionary."

Daisy's eyes followed Turner's glance toward the windows, noticing the additional security for the first time. "Yeah... I was going to ask about that. What's going on? Why all the extra security?"

Agent Turner set her coffee aside and pulled out her laptop, laying it on the table alongside a few files. "We'll get to that in a moment," she said, her voice taking on a more serious tone. "There are some updates on the investigation, and I need to share them with you."

Daisy's pulse quickened as Turner's expression darkened. She sat up straighter, watching closely as Turner opened her laptop and pulled up several documents.

"The cars at the Tennessee 400," Agent Turner began. "It was an AI-generated malware attack."

Daisy blinked, her brow furrowing in confusion. "Malware? Like… computer viruses?"

Agent Turner nodded. "Exactly. Someone used advanced AI to create a virus that sent fake commands to the cars, making them all stall at the same time."

Daisy's eyes widened as she tried to wrap her head around it. "How does that even happen? I don't get it—how could malware infect race cars?"

Agent Turner leaned forward slightly, choosing her words carefully. "Well, you know cars way better than me but from what my tech agent tells me, the car computers got a software update before the race. It was during the update that the virus got into the cars and hijacked the communication system."

Daisy sat back, absorbing the explanation. "So whoever did this… did they send the cars a command to stall?"

"Yes," Agent Turner said. " And just as quickly as it appeared, the virus wiped itself clean, leaving almost no trace."

Daisy stared at the table, disbelief flickering across her face. "Why would someone do that? What's the point?"

Agent Turner sighed, her fingers tapping lightly on the laptop. "We believe it's connected to everything else that's happened—Kelli's attack, Tommy Crow crashing into you. And… the hacking of your medical records."

Daisy's heart raced. "My medical records? I didn't know they were hacked."

"Yes," Turner said, her voice calm but firm. "Our cyberteam found similar code patterns in the virus and the hacks into your medical records. We also think this person has hacked into the medical records of others to use as leverage."

Daisy's face drained of color. "Do you know who it is?"

Agent Turner's eyes narrowed as she leaned in, her voice low. "We have a strong suspicion. And we're coming to you first with this information to fill in the blanks."

Daisy's fingers tightened around her coffee mug as she waited, her anxiety building.

Agent Turner turned her laptop around, the screen displaying a face that Daisy hadn't seen in years. "Daisy," Turner said slowly, "do you know this man?"

Daisy's eyes widened, and she pushed her chair back, her voice barely above a whisper. "That's Lumen Ross."

Agent Turner nodded, watching Daisy's reaction carefully. "Yes. Lumen Ross. He's our number one suspect. It all leads back to him."

Daisy's stomach dropped, a wave of nausea and anger washing over her. She took a deep breath, trying to steady herself. "Are you saying... Lumen is behind everything that happened? Tommy, Kelli, the race?"

Agent Turner's gaze was steady. "Yes, Daisy. And we don't think he's done."

Daisy stood abruptly, pushing her chair back as she paced across the room. "I need to call Morgan," she said, her voice shaking. "I need to warn her."

"Daisy, wait," Turner said, standing as well. "There's more I need to ask you—"

But Daisy turned toward the door, her mind focused solely on her sister. As she moved through the house, Jackson, Riley, and Papa Joe appeared, their faces lined with concern. Jackson reached her first, his hands gently gripping her shoulders. "Daisy, what's going on? What did Agent Turner say?"

Daisy's voice trembled as she looked into Jackson's worried eyes. "It's Lumen Ross, Jackson. He's behind everything. I need to call Morgan."

Chapter 19

Agent Turner, stood in the kitchen, sensing the situation spiraling out of control. She turned to Joe Wyatt, her expression tense. "Joe, I need to get Daisy back. I need her to talk about Lumen."

She watched Mr. Wyatt walk over to a small wet bar in the corner of the kitchen. He poured two glasses of whiskey, bringing them back to the table. He slid one across to Agent Turner and took a sip from the other.

"Do you drink, Agent Turner?" he asked.

"Not while I'm on duty," she replied, her brow furrowing.

She watched him take another sip, sensing he was gearing up for a shift in conversation.

"So, Agent Turner," Joe began, his voice steady but cautious, "what exactly do you know about Lumen Ross?"

Agent Turner leaned back slightly in her chair, clasping her hands together on the table. "So based on my initial questioning of racing officials, I learned he was expelled from the racing association after a failed drug and alcohol test. There were reports of erratic driving on the track, and from what I gathered, the racing association had enough after a string of incidents. His sponsors pulled out their support. Lumen did the required rehab and his license was reinstated. But then he went back to his old ways of reckless driving and off-track antics. The racing association ran a test again and found alcohol and drugs in his system. After that, he was gone for good."

Joe nodded, swirling the whiskey in his glass. "That much is true. But there's a lot more to it. More than racing's official story, at least."

Agent Tuner took notice of Joe tightening his hand around the glass. His gaze didn't leave the whiskey. "Carson Kray, Daisy's father... he did what any father would do. He was protecting her." His voice was rough like gravel being stirred.

Agent Turner waited, sensing the gravity of what was coming. "What do you mean by protecting her, Joe?"

Joe exhaled deeply, his broad shoulders slumping slightly. "It started when Daisy was still young, just getting into racing. Lumen... well, he was always trouble. He had this wild reputation, both on the track and off it. He rubbed Daisy's car a few times during races…"

Agent Turner interrupted. "Rubbed?"

"Yeah, it's when a car makes contact with another car without causing a crash."

Agent Turner nodded her head and encouraged Joe to continue.

"Well, Lumen started calling Daisy out in the media. He was a bully. Daisy dealt with it well, which seemed to get into Lumen's craw. Things escalated when Daisy overtook the lead from Lumen at Talladega, passing him on the inside last turn. He didn't see it coming. It was Daisy's first win." Joe smiled, recalling the victory.

Agent Turner jotted down some notes from Joe's story. "I assume Lumen's ego took a beating after that loss."

"Oh and how! He got it from other drivers, the press, and the media. He was furious." Joe stopped for a moment as he took a sigh. "Which brings me to when things went from bad to worse between Lumen and the Krays."

Agent Turner put her pen and notebook down and focused only on Joe.

"Joe, tell me what happened. What did you mean earlier about Carson Kray protecting Daisy?"

Joe's expression tightened. "It was a couple of weeks after Daisy beat Lumen at Talladega. There was an after-party that all the teams attended. Lumen cornered Daisy. Tried to kiss her. She pushed him away but he tried again, pretty aggressively from what I understand. Daisy punched him in the face and kneed him in the groin."

Agent Turner's eyes widened slightly, a mix of shock and admiration flashing across her face for a split second before she composed herself. "Daisy did that to Lumen?"

Joe nodded. "Daisy was always one to stand up for herself, especially against someone like Lumen. Her father had her in self-defense and judo classes the moment he knew she was going to drive race cars against a bunch of testosterone-filled boys."

Agent Turner shook her head and empathized with being a woman in a male-dominated field. "Keep going, Joe."

Joe sighed, leaning back in his chair. "When Carson found out what happened, he lost it. He insisted on a private meeting with racing's top brass, but all Lumen got was a slap on the wrist."

"So, what did Carson do?" Agent Turner asked, her voice low, anticipating the revelation.

She could see the hesitation in his face. He reached for the whiskey, took another sip, and set the glass down with a thud.

"Carson was a man who believed in justice. But more than that, he was a father who'd do anything to protect his daughter. Lumen had already failed a drug test before, and under the racing association's rules, one more slip-up would mean a permanent ban. Carson knew that, and he also knew Lumen's weakness—his drinking. So he set Lumen him up."

Agent Turner's eyes widened. "How so?"

Joe rubbed the hair of his beard. "Carson found out about a gentlemen's club Lumen frequented with locations in some of the same cities as the races and confirmed that Lumen would drink alcohol at these clubs, many times less than twelve hours before a race, which violated racing association rules. One weekend Carson anonymously leaked this to the media, who showed up to the club with cameras and smartphones. To ensure the final nail in the coffin of Lumen's racing career, Carson paid someone off to slip an Ativan into Lumen's drink. Just enough to show up in his system."

Agent Turner processed the implications of Joe's revelation. The weight of the information hit her, and she could feel the pieces falling into place. "So, Carson orchestrated the entire thing. He made sure Lumen would fail a drug alcohol test."

"Yes," Joe admitted, his voice barely above a whisper. "The racing association had no choice but to test him, and when the results came back—alcohol and drugs in his system—Lumen was finished. Carson pushed hard for the expulsion, and with his spotless reputation, the racing association couldn't ignore him."

Agent Turner sat back, absorbing the enormity of what she had just learned. "Carson had that kind of influence."

Joe nodded, his voice softening. "Carson was a man who always played by the rules, but when it came to protecting his family, he'd do anything. He wasn't proud of what he did, but he thought it was the only way to keep Daisy safe. He also truly believed Lumen was dangerous to all drivers."

Agent Turner paused, her mind racing. "And you think Lumen found out about this somehow? He knows Carson was behind it?"

Joe's brow tensed, his face lined with uncertainty. "I don't know for sure. But if I had to guess, yeah. I think Lumen figured it out. Lumen couldn't get his revenge on Carson, so he's coming for Daisy now."

Agent Turner looked down at the files on the table, the significance of the situation pressing on her. "If Lumen found out that Carson set him up, it would explain why he was going to such lengths to come after Daisy."

"Revenge," Joe murmured, shaking his head. "Lumen's always been the kind of man who couldn't let things go. This isn't just about racing. It's personal. It always has been."

Agent Turner let out a long breath, absorbing the revelation. "I understood Carson to be well-respected, a clean-cut guy. Sure didn't expect this."

"There's something else you should know, Agent Turner." Joe held back for a moment, his voice growing heavier with the next confession. "Daisy… she never knew. She doesn't know that her father set up Lumen. As far as she's concerned, Lumen's red devil ways caught up to him and he was expelled."

Agent Turner's brows shot up in surprise. "How long have you been keeping this from her?"

Joe looked down at his hands, the burden of his guilt visible in his weathered features. "Too long. I should've told her years ago, but I couldn't bear the thought of tarnishing Carson's image in her eyes. Then time passed and no one heard from Lumen again, until now."

Agent Turner pulled her chair in closer and leaned into the table. "And how do you know all of this, Joe?"

Agent Turner watched Joe's hands tremble as they rested on his knees. He stared down at the floor, his gaze deliberately avoiding hers as if he couldn't bear to meet her eyes. "It was Randy, one of my ranch wranglers, who drugged Lumen," he finally admitted, his voice barely a whisper.

Agent Turner studied Joe's troubled expression. She could sense the guilt and conflict within him, the burden of years of silence finally unraveling before her eyes. "Why did you decide to get involved?"

Joe looked frustrated. "Like I said, Lumen was trouble for everyone. He had some fights with Jackson and made some dangerous moves against him in some races. About a dozen other drivers could tell you the same thing. I can't tell you the number of times Lumen was fined, but that didn't matter. What the racing association won't admit to you is that they like a bad guy in the mix. Every good story needs a villain, and Lumen was racing's bad boy. His antics and wondering what the red devil would do next brought a lot of fans out to the speedway, upped broadcast viewership and sold a heck of a lot of merch. Carson and I had talked about our mutual frustration over Lumen's behavior many times. We thought some sort of intervention would have to happen to force Lumen out since the racing association would drag their feet knowing the financial impact it could have to let him go. That's why he came to me to help. And I was all in."

Agent Turner listened intently, absorbing each word as it painted a clearer picture of the tangled web spun by Joe Wyatt and Carson Kray. Silence settled over the room for a moment as she contemplated the consequences. Then, she met his eyes with a steady gaze. "How long do you think you can keep this from her?"

Joe sighed, rubbing the back of his neck. "I can't anymore, but I don't want her to find out from you or anyone else. I need to be the one to tell her. She deserves to hear it from me."

Agent Turner considered his words carefully. She knew the situation was delicate and that Daisy deserved to know the truth, but revealing too much could jeopardize the investigation. She could also see the tension on Joe's face and knew he was hoping for her trust and discretion. "Look, Joe, it's not my job to keep secrets from Daisy, especially when it pertains to an ongoing investigation. But…" she paused, weighing her next words, "I can take the evening for further investigation."

Joe nodded slowly, his gratitude evident in his eyes. "Thank you, Agent Turner. I'll tell her myself after you leave. I just need a little more time to figure out how."

Agent Turner leaned back in her chair, watching him with a mixture of empathy and determination. "You better tell her, Joe. This could come out any minute. And she deserves to know the truth, especially with everything that's going on."

"I know," Joe murmured. He drained the last of his whiskey, the glass thudding softly against the table. "I'll tell her. It's just... hard. She looked up to Carson like he was invincible."

"Neither Morgan nor Jackson knows either, do they?" Agent Turner asked, her voice quieter now.

"No, they don't," Joe confirmed, rubbing his temples as if the memories themselves pained him. "Carson was a friend. He did what he did to protect his daughter, and I understand why he did it. I would have done it myself."

Agent Turner sighed, crossing her arms. "I get it, Joe. Honestly, I'd probably do the same in his shoes. But this is going to blow up when it comes out. The sooner you tell her, the better."

Joe nodded again, quieter this time. "I'll tell her."

Agent Turner stood up, closed her laptop, and gathered her files. "You don't have much time. Lumen is out there, and we don't know what he's planning next. You need to make sure Daisy knows what she's up against."

Joe glanced down at the whiskey glass in his hand before setting it aside, a deep sadness settling in his eyes. "I know. I just hope I'm not too late."

The agent nodded solemnly, giving him a final look of understanding. "Me too."

Chapter 20

Daisy's boots shuffled through the grass as she walked beside Jackson, her phone clutched tightly in her hand. They were headed toward an open clearing just past the horse pasture, the distant silhouette of a dense forest beyond it. Two FBI agents trailed behind them, their acute eyes scanning the horizon, a quiet tension between them. The crisp air smelled of pine and fresh earth, but Daisy's mind was far from serene. She kept tapping the screen of her phone, desperately trying to get a message through to her sister. The worry in her chest clenched like a vice with every unanswered call.

"Come on, Morgan, pick up," Daisy muttered under her breath, as she fired off yet another text.

"She's not answering," Daisy said aloud, her voice tinged with panic. She shot Jackson a glance, her brow furrowed in frustration. "Why isn't she answering? She always picks up for me."

Jackson, who had been trying to reach Roger, lowered his phone with a grimace. "I'm not getting anything from Roger either," he said, his calm voice belying the growing concern Daisy saw in his eyes.

Daisy felt Jackson's arm wrap around her shoulders, trying to soothe her. "Look, it's probably just a reception issue. We're out here on the ranch, and you know how the signal can be spotty."

Daisy wasn't convinced. Her mind was racing, jumping from worry to anger in quick succession. She stopped walking for a moment, turning to face Jackson fully. "It's not just the signal, Jackson. It's Lumen. He's behind everything—Kelli, the race, everything! And now my sister isn't answering, and I can't—"

"Hey," Jackson interrupted gently, stepping closer and softening his voice. "I get it. I'm worried too. But freaking out right now isn't going to help. Let's keep moving. Take a breath. We'll figure it out."

Daisy inhaled sharply, running a hand through her hair, but the anxiety twisting in her gut wasn't easing up. "I just need to know she's alright. After everything Lumen did—he's capable of anything."

Jackson gave her shoulder a reassuring squeeze. "Just keep walking with me. The agents are on high alert."

As they walked, a sudden cold breeze rustled through the trees, making the hairs on the back of Daisy's neck rise. She glanced over her shoulder, but there was nothing—just the empty horizon and the quiet crunch of the agents' footsteps. Still, something felt off.

They had just entered the wooded area when Daisy's phone buzzed. Her heart leaped, thinking it might be Morgan. But as she glanced at the screen, her blood ran cold. It wasn't Morgan.

Daisy pressed the phone to her ear, her pulse quickening. "Agent Turner?"

Agent Turner's voice crackled through the speaker, low and urgent. "Daisy, we've got a situation. A vehicle was just clocked going over 100 miles per hour and has made it onto Jackson's property. It's coming your way—"

Before Daisy could respond, the two FBI agents stiffened, their headsets buzzing with the same information.

"Get her back to the ranch!" one of the agents barked, grabbing Daisy by the arm and pulling her behind them.

Jackson shielded Daisy with his body as they began to sprint back the way they came. The sound of their footsteps echoed against the stillness of the woods. They had barely made it a few yards when the first arrow whizzed through the air and struck one of the agents in the leg. The agent crumpled with a pained grunt, clutching his leg as blood began to seep through his pants.

"Go! Get her out of here!" the second agent screamed, only to be silenced by another arrow that lodged itself deep into his thigh. He collapsed next to his partner, both of them yelling into their radios, "We're down! We're down! Get backup!"

Panic surged through Daisy as Jackson grabbed her hand, pulling her faster toward the ranch. But before they could get far, a low, menacing whirring filled the air. From the edge of the woods, a sleek, red sports car roared into view, its engine purring like a predator stalking its prey.

The car skidded to a halt directly in their path, its completely darkened windows offering no clue as to who—or what—was inside. As Daisy and Jackson froze, the passenger door swung open with a slow, deliberate hiss, revealing an empty seat.

"There's no driver…" Daisy whispered, her voice tinged with disbelief.

Jackson's grip on her hand hardened, his fingers locking around hers as if to anchor both of them. "Daisy, we need to—"

Suddenly, from the shadows of the trees, a tall man dressed in head-to-toe camouflage appeared, his face obscured by a mask. He moved with terrifying speed, tackling Jackson to the ground and sending him sprawling.

Daisy screamed, instinctively backing away, but the man was too fast. He lunged for her, forcing her into the passenger seat of the car with brutal efficiency. The door slammed shut behind her, locking her inside.

"Jackson!" Daisy yelled, pounding on the window as she watched Jackson struggle with the masked man outside. Before she could do anything, an unyielding seatbelt snapped across Daisy's chest and abdomen, causing an immediate shot of pain that tore through her body. The belt dug into the spot where she'd had her surgery, the tightness pressing cruelly against her most vulnerable area. It wasn't just the pressure; it was as though the car itself had somehow known where to target her.

The car zoomed away at top speed. Daisy's vision blurred for a moment as she bit down hard on her lip, trying to keep from crying out. Her breath came in short, ragged bursts, and every attempt to wriggle free sent fresh waves of agony through her side. She tried to arch her back, desperate for relief, but the seatbelt only tightened further, locking her in place like a vice.

Then she heard it—a voice creeping out of the speakers, low and taunting.

"Oh, don't hurt yourself, Daisy. I wouldn't want that... yet."

Her head snapped up, her heart pounding in her chest as the voice crawled through the air, familiar in a way that made her stomach churn. Lumen. But before she could react, the windshield in front of her flickered to life, the clear glass transforming into a high-tech screen, the glow casting a cold light over her trapped figure.

Lumen's face filled the screen, his dark eyes narrowing in sick amusement as he watched her struggle. His lips curled into a smirk, a cigar hanging lazily from the corner of his mouth, wisps of smoke trailing from the digital image. His gaze, cold and predatory, seemed to look right through her as if he could feel the agony she was in.

"Hurts, doesn't it?" His voice oozed with mock sympathy, the sound filling every corner of the car. "You're in pain, Daisy. I can see it. That's the thing about technology… It's very smart. Knows exactly where to hit you hardest."

Every inch of Daisy's skin crawled under Lumen's watchful eyes. The car wasn't just a cage; it was an extension of Lumen's sadistic control.

Her vision blurred again, the pain now mingling with panic as she stared at the screen. His face, larger than life, smirked down at her like he had all the time in the world to watch her suffer. His voice echoed inside her head, heightening the sense of dread.

"You've caused me so much trouble, Daisy. So much trouble. But now…" He paused, leaning closer to the camera, his dark eyes gleaming with malice. "Now it's time we had a real conversation, don't you think?"

Chapter 21

Daisy's heart pounded harder, her body slick with cold sweat as she fought to keep her composure. She could see he wanted to drag out the terror, to watch her break under the crushing force of fear.

She couldn't let him. Not like this.

"Still smoking those cigars Lumen? You know those things can kill you." Daisy fired, determined to stay strong amid the chaos that surrounded her.

Lumen snickered and took a long drag from his cigar, the smoke swirling around his face before dissipating into the digital wind. "I've been told that before," he replied, his voice filled with sadistic pleasure. "But I suppose it's all part of the thrill, isn't it? And speaking of thrills, it is thrilling to see you again. Even in pain, you look stunning."

Lumen's comments made Daisy's skin crawl. The sound of his voice unleashed a mix of determination and anger within her. "I'm getting out of this car, Lumen" Daisy growled, her voice low and lethal despite the pain that tore through her side. "And when I do, I'll bury you so deep, no one will ever have to endure your twisted games again."

"Oh, Daisy," he cooed, his voice slick with condescension. "You can't even move. Do you really think you're in control here? No, sweetheart. This is *my* game. And I'm just getting started."

Daisy's mind was racing as she fought through the pain. Summoning her strength, she forced the words out, her voice strained but determined.

"So if this is about me, why Kelli?" she demanded, as she tried to push through the pain in her side. "She had nothing to do with you. Why drag her into this? And Tommy—why him?"

Lumen's face flickered on the screen, his expression darkening. He tilted his head, considering her question with a twisted smile.

"Kelli Foster," Lumen began, his voice slow, deliberate. "She was the perfect leverage. I know what she means to you, Daisy. I knew she isn't just a teammate. She's like family. Hurting her was a sure way to make you suffer. To make you feel guilty, to see someone you care about torn apart because of you. That's a pain that lingers, doesn't it?"

Daisy's heart pounded, each beat a reminder of the bond she shared with Kelli. The thought of her lying in a hospital bed, injured because of Lumen's madness, made her stomach turn.

"You went after her because you thought your insane actions would make me feel guilty?" Daisy asked, her voice trembling with a mix of fury and pain.

Lumen's smile widened, his teeth flashing in the dim glow of the car's dashboard lights.

"Exactly. You see, Daisy, it was never just about hurting you physically. No, that's too easy. But watching you suffer emotionally, watching you wrestle with guilt? That's satisfying. Kelli was the perfect choice—your dear friend, your mentee, practically another sister. I knew it would break you in ways nothing else could."

Daisy's hands clenched into fists as she glared at the screen, her knuckles white from the pressure. "You're sick," she spat, her voice low and filled with venom. "Using someone like that—"

"And as for Tommy," Lumen interrupted, his voice growing colder, more detached, "he was the perfect pawn. Desperate, drowning in medical debt from treatments that didn't work… he had nothing to lose. It was almost poetic, really. He wanted to go out with a bang, leave his mark, and I offered him the perfect opportunity."

Daisy felt her stomach twist. "You made a deal with a dying man," she said, the realization sinking in.

Lumen's smirk returned, more terrorizing than before. "He knew he didn't have much time left, Daisy. All he needed was a nudge. I gave him a deal. In exchange for doing me a favor, he'd get the kind of attention he always craved. It didn't take much to convince him."

"A deal with the devil," Daisy repeated, her voice dripping with disgust.

Lumen chuckled darkly, the sound reverberating through the speakers. "Yes, and like any good deal with the devil, the price was steep. But Tommy didn't care. He was dying anyway—he just wanted security for his family and to be remembered. And what better way than by taking down Daisy Kray?"

Daisy's mind raced as she struggled to process Lumen's words, his cruelty pressing down on her.

"You used a dying man and destroyed someone I loved—all just to get to me," she said, her voice cracking.

Lumen's eyes gleamed with warped satisfaction. "And it worked, didn't it? Kelli is broken, Tommy is dead, and here you are—trapped, bleeding, and forced to face the truth. The sins of your father have come back to haunt you, Daisy."

At the mention of her father, Daisy's breath caught in her throat. "What do you mean by that?"

Lumen's smile vanished, replaced by something colder, more sinister. "Your father," he sneered, his voice dripping with disgust, "destroyed my one true love. Racing. Your father made sure I was expelled, made sure I'd never set foot on a track again. Do you know what that's like, Daisy? To have everything you love ripped away?"

Daisy shook her head, the rage rising in her like a tidal wave. "You did that to yourself, Lumen! You were reckless, dangerous. Everyone saw it. My father had nothing to do with you getting kicked off the track—it was your actions that got you expelled."

Lumen's gaze flickered. For a brief moment, his calm façade cracked, and a hint of rage broke through. Then he quickly composed himself, his smile returning, though this time, it was colder than before.

"Ah, Daisy," he said softly, almost pityingly. "So you really don't know, do you?"

Daisy felt a sense of alarm in anticipation of Lumen's revelation. "Know what?" she asked, as her voice wavered.

Lumen leaned closer to the screen, his eyes narrowing with savage delight as he spoke. "Your father wasn't the saint you thought he was. I suspected for years that Carson Kray had a hand in my downfall. I recently found the proof I needed—your father set me up."

Daisy's pulse raced, her mind in disbelief. "You're lying," she snapped, though even as she said it, doubt began to creep in. "My father wouldn't—"

Lumen chuckled darkly. "Oh, I'm sure he let you believe that, but Carson wasn't always the hero. You see, Daisy, your father knew one more infraction would get me expelled for life. So, he arranged it. That drug and alcohol test I failed before the race? Carson orchestrated the whole thing! Had me tailed, tainted my drink, and leaked it to the media! The man was ruthless when it came to kicking me out, especially after our special moment together when you broke my jaw."

"You deserved the beating I gave you, Lumen," Daisy sneered as she looked into his image on the screen. "And if my father did anything, it was just to protect the other drivers from your insanity."

Lumen's smile widened, his satisfaction clear. "You'll come to terms with the truth soon enough," he said, his tone patronizing. "He was willing to do whatever it took to take me down. And now, I'm doing the same to you."

"You're lying," she hissed again, her voice more desperate now, but Lumen only laughed, his cruel amusement filling every inch of the car.

"I'm afraid the truth stings, doesn't it?" he taunted.

Lumen's words echoed in her mind like a slow, torturous drip. Was it true? Could her father have set Lumen up? No, she couldn't believe it. Not now. Not when everything was crumbling around her. The nagging doubt pressed at her, gnawing at her already fragile heart.

"Oh, by the way," Lumen's voice filled with sarcasm, "how's your older sister been lately?"

Daisy's body froze. She stared at the screen as anger and fear tangled together inside of her.

"What did you just say?"

Lumen's eyes glittered with sadistic pleasure. "Come now, Daisy. You didn't think I'd forget dear Morgan, did you?"

The screen flickered, and to Daisy's horror, a live feed of Morgan's house appeared. Her sister, looking pale and tired, lay in bed, clearly worried and alone. Daisy felt the blood drain from her face, dread settling like a stone in her gut.

"I hacked into her medical records, of course," Lumen continued gleefully. "High-risk pregnancy… quite delicate, really. It would be such a shame if something happened to her and your precious nephew-to-be."

Daisy's eyes brimmed with tears. She couldn't comprehend the depth of Lumen's evil, how far he was willing to go. Her mind screamed at her to focus, to fight, but the thought of her sister and unborn nephew in danger made her feel like she was breaking.

Lumen's voice shifted to a mocking tone, gushing with false sympathy. "Oh, that's right. The doctor's notes said Morgan didn't want to know the sex of the baby, did she? Well, surprise, Daisy. It's a boy."

Tears she had been holding back finally started to spill over. Lumen lived up to his reputation as the red devil in incomprehensible ways. She had to find a way out of this, for her, for Morgan, for her family. She gritted her teeth, allowing Lumen to continue his vile monologue while she surveyed her surroundings, desperate to spot any weakness in the car's structure.

She took note of a crack at the bottom of the passenger window. A tiny flaw, but enough to give her hope for a possible exit strategy. She rubbed her head against the headrest, calculating. It felt loose enough—if she could get it out, she might have a shot but she had to get the seatbelts off of her. She decided she had to make Lumen believe she was unwell.

Lumen, clearly irritated by her lack of response, raised his voice. "I'm talking to you, Daisy! Pay attention to me!"

His shout pierced her eardrums, but it was exactly what she needed. The distraction allowed her to move her head just enough to get a better feel for the gap between the headrest and the seat.

"Lu...men," Daisy slurred, letting her body sag forward as if she was losing consciousness. She rolled her eyes back dramatically, letting out a fake gasp, her breaths becoming more labored. She made herself twitch, a violent, erratic jerk.

"What are you doing?" Lumen's voice shifted, with the beginnings of panic. "Oh no, Daisy. You're not dying on me yet."

She let her body hang limp in the seat, her chest rising and falling in exaggerated, wheezing breaths. "I... I can't... breathe..." she gasped, slumping to the side.

"Dammit!" Lumen snarled. "Wake up!"

Daisy cracked her eyelids just enough to see Lumen frantically typing on his tablet. Her heart pounded in anticipation while her muscles tensed beneath the pain. Then, with a sharp click, the seatbelt suddenly loosened.

Without hesitation, she turned towards the back of the passenger seat and yanked the headrest out, exposing the hardened steel rods that had helped keep the headrest in place. She swung the headrest toward the window with all the strength she could muster. The first blow sent a satisfying crack through the glass, but she wasn't done. Fueled by adrenaline and sheer desperation, she struck again and again. The window started to shatter outward, sending shards of tempered glass flying into the wind.

"Daisy!" Lumen's voice thundered through the speakers as he accelerated the car, trying to shake her back into submission.

The wind whipped at her face, the car's speed making it nearly impossible to hold on. She knew that jumping would likely kill her, but she couldn't stay inside. She had to find a way out—her only option was to get to the roof. With every ounce of strength left in her, she managed to get her torso out of what was left of the passenger side window and clawed her way up.

As she pulled herself out the window, a large black truck sped up alongside her.

Jackson drove, his face tight with fear and determination. Beside him, Agent Turner leaned out of the window, shouting over the roaring wind. "Jump, Daisy! We've got you!"

The truck's cab aligned with the car for just a split second, but it was enough. Summoning the last reserves of her energy, Daisy threw herself toward the truck's open cab.

Riley, along with two FBI agents, reached out, their hands grasping for hers.

They caught her just in time, pulling her into the cab. Daisy collapsed onto the floor, her chest heaving as she lay on her back, covered in cuts from the shattered glass. Blood trickled from her arms and legs, and the sharp pain from her surgery wound screamed with every breath she took.

She heard the truck screeching to a halt as the SUVs behind them continued their pursuit of Lumen's car. Daisy felt the agony of her now open surgery wound bleeding as Jackson and Agent Turner made their way into the back of the truck.

"Daisy, stay with me," Jackson whispered, his voice thick with fear. He grabbed her hand, squeezing it tight, refusing to let her drift away. " You're going to be okay."

Through the haze of pain, Daisy managed to look at him, her voice barely more than a whisper. "Morgan... you have to get to Morgan. She's in danger."

Agent Turner, still catching her breath from the chaos, knelt beside them. "Daisy, we have an entire team with Morgan and Roger. She's safe."

Daisy shook her head weakly, her eyes clouded with doubt. "There was an FBI team here too... and look what happened."

Her eyes closed for a moment, the exhaustion weighing her down. The world felt heavy, distant. She heard Agent Turner calling for a helicopter, but the thought of being lifted into the air again was too much.

"Not... another... helicopter," Daisy muttered, her lips barely moving.

Jackson leaned closer, his voice soft but urgent. "Yes, and this time no one is stopping me from going in there with you."

Daisy's lips twitched into a faint smile before the pain and exhaustion pulled her back under. The last thing she felt before everything faded was the warmth of Jackson's hand holding hers, the one thing tethering her to the world as darkness surrounded her.

Chapter 22

The barn was quiet except for the occasional rustle of hay as Chief shifted his weight, his warm breath huffing softly in the air. Daisy leaned her head back against the wooden wall of Chief's stall and closed her eyes, willing herself to breathe through the storm that raged inside her. The betrayal, the fear, the constant pressure—it was overwhelming. Chief stood near her, his massive body a comforting presence as he occasionally nudged her shoulder with his soft nose. She absentmindedly stroked his mane, her fingers tangling in the coarse hair as she let the warmth of the animal soothe her. The quiet rustling of hay beneath Chief's hooves and the steady sound of his breathing were soothing, at a time when everything else in her life had come crashing down, and she didn't know how to pick up the pieces.

Daisy's mind shifted to the presence of the FBI, the agents stationed outside every door, every window. At first, she'd been relieved, thankful for the protection. But now, after everything, she felt like she was suffocating. Their presence was a reminder of her new reality—that she was being hunted. It was part of why she'd come out to the barn. She needed to feel some sense of freedom, even if it was only here, sitting with Chief in the quiet.

The past few days had been a whirlwind. Her mind drifted, replaying everything that had happened. Just a few days ago, she narrowly escaped Lumen's self-driving death trap. The FBI captured the car about 20 miles from Jackson's ranch. Although equipped with the most technologically advanced defense mechanisms, the feds shot out the tires enough times to finally stop it from running. Agent Turner reported that a team of mechanics and engineers were studying the car to find any information on Lumen's possible location.

The glass cuts and injuries Daisy suffered seemed like nothing compared to the emotional toll she was carrying. At the hospital, the doctors had tended to her, and everyone had been shocked at how well she recovered physically. Yet no one could see the deeper scars, the ones left on her heart.

Her mind jumped to Papa Joe's confession—the revelation that Carson, her father, *had* set up Lumen Ross. She'd spent years believing her father was a man of integrity, that everything Lumen had claimed was a lie, but now… she knew the truth. She could understand her father's desire to protect his family, but how much was too far? Her father's actions had set everything in motion, leading to this mess, leading to Lumen's vendetta. Did that make her father responsible for all of this?

Even Papa Joe had admitted to being part of the plan. He had arranged for Randy, the family's trusted wrangler, to slip drugs into Lumen's drink.

Randy was the biggest heartache of them all.... Daisy grimaced at the thought of him. The wrangler who had worked for the Wyatt family for over 15 years had betrayed them. And yet he had been the one who shot the arrows at the FBI and pushed Daisy into Lumen's car. After being captured soon after the driverless car took Daisy, Randy admitted to the FBI that he had been contacting Lumen with updates about Daisy's whereabouts at the ranch on an encrypted phone because he'd been blackmailed by Lumen. Lumen had threatened to steal Randy's identity, to ruin him, and he had caved under the pressure. Daisy understood fear, but this kind of betrayal? It cut deep.

She was tired. Tired of the constant fear. Tired of being a pawn in Lumen's twisted game. And worse, terrified—for herself, her sister, and her sister's baby. Morgan had been moved to the hospital, and put on bed rest, because of Lumen's threat against her baby. Her sister was supposed to be enjoying the final months of her pregnancy, not worrying about the possibility of Lumen Ross causing complications.

As these recollections burdened Daisy's mind, the creak of the barn door caught her attention, and she glanced up to see Riley stepping into the barn.

"Hey," Riley said softly as she approached. "I figured I'd find you here."

Daisy nodded, not trusting her voice to come out steady.

Riley stood beside her. Daisy felt Riley's sharp eyes sweeping over her. "You know, I've seen you in some low points before, but this…" Riley let out a small sigh. "This is different. You're different. Talk to me, Daisy."

Daisy shook her head, tears stinging the back of her eyes. "I don't even know where to start, Riley. It's like everything's falling apart."

Riley opened her arms signaling Daisy to lean on her for a comforting hug. "I know it feels that way, but you're not alone in this. You've got people who care about you—Jackson, me, Roger, the whole racing community. Hell, even the FBI's got your back."

Daisy let out a shaky breath. "But Lumen… he's still out there. And Morgan…"

"Morgan's safe," Riley reassured her. "The FBI's got her locked down tighter than Fort Knox at that hospital. Nobody's getting to her or that baby."

Daisy wanted to believe it. She wanted to feel that sense of security but after everything that had happened, it was hard to trust in anything anymore.

Riley pulled out her phone, opening the notes section as Daisy sensed a shift in the topic of conversation.

"So I came out here with some racing news. I just got off a call with the racing association. They've been working with the FBI and all kinds of tech wizards. They developed this patch that'll prevent what Lumen did to the cars from happening again. They've tested it and are continuing to trial-run different scenarios. Plus, there's an enhanced warning system now, something that'll alert the teams if anything like that tries to breach the system again."

"Really?" Daisy's voice was soft, a glimmer of hope surfacing.

"Yeah," Riley said, nodding. "They're hoping to get racing going again soon. It's still dependent on finding Lumen, of course, but they're working on it."

Daisy felt a heaviness in her chest, thinking about all the drivers, teams, and racing association employees who couldn't do their jobs because of a deranged man's obsession. "Everything is on hold because of all this. I feel awful Riley."

"It's not your fault, Daisy," Riley said firmly. "Everyone knows this is Lumen's doing. The other drivers—hell, the whole community—they're rallying behind you. They're all sending their support. Roger, Jackson, and I can't go five minutes without getting a message from someone asking about you. They want to get back to racing, but they want to do it safely. No one blames you for any of this."

Daisy managed a small, grateful smile. "Thanks, Riley. That means a lot."

"Oh, and by the way, Daisy… I took another look at the GT500. That beauty's in top shape. The brakes are solid, the engine's roaring, and the gear shift is excellent. It's ready for you whenever you are."

Daisy's smile grew a little wider at the mention of her car. "Thanks for looking after it."

"Of course," Riley said, standing up and brushing some hay off her jeans. "You're gonna get through this, you know. You've got more fight in you than anyone I know."

Just then, Jackson entered the barn. Riley and Daisy exchanged another hug and Riley stepped away, nodding to Jackson as she headed for the door of the barn.

"I'll leave you two," Riley said, pausing as she passed Jackson just long enough to whisper, "Take care of our girl, okay?"

Jackson nodded at Riley as she left.

"That's the first time I've seen you smile like that in days, Daisy," he said, his voice deep and relieved.

He walked into the stall and gently ran his hand over Chief's mane as he stood next to Daisy.

"Mind if we sit?" Jackson asked.

Daisy shook her head. "Of course."

As they perched next to each other on a large haystack near Chief, Daisy relished the warmth of Jackson's presence. They remained quiet for a few moments, taking in the sounds of the soft shuffling of Chief's hooves and the distant rustle of wind outside the barn. It was Jackson who eventually broke their silence.

"Daisy, I feel like I've failed you," Jackson said quietly. "Randy… I had no idea he'd been feeding Lumen information. I should've known. I should've protected you from him pushing you into that car."

Daisy reached over, gently touching his face. "You couldn't have known, Jackson. Randy… he was like family. And you *did* protect me. You're my hero! No one else could have driven that truck like that. You saved me."

He leaned into her hand for a moment before he spoke again. "I still wish I could've done more. But what really hurts is knowing you're carrying so much guilt and pain about all this. None of this is your fault."

Daisy's eyes filled with tears, and her defenses started to crumble. "It's not just Lumen. It's my father."

Jackson leaned closer, his hand brushing her hair back from her face, his thumb gently tracing her cheek. "Even the smartest of men can't always predict outcomes, Daisy. Your father did what he did because he wanted to protect you. I understand that. And Lumen was already on his way out, no matter what your father did. Lumen was dangerous and reckless. It was inevitable."

Daisy's heart softened at Jackson's words. She hadn't expected him to understand her so deeply, to offer her this kind of grace. It was moments like this when she realized just how much she needed him. How much he grounded her. She turned slightly towards him, their faces now just inches apart. Her lips trembled as she spoke.

"I don't know what I'd do without you," she whispered, tears rolling down her cheeks.

Jackson wiped away her tears with his thumb. "You'll never have to find out," he said softly.

Their eyes locked and in that moment, Daisy knew without a doubt that Jackson would always be there for her, no matter what.

Jackson took her hand and kissed it gently. "Please tell me what you need. Don't be afraid to ask," he whispered to her.

Daisy felt a weight pressing down on her chest, the burden of everything she had been carrying for so long. Ever since she lost her parents, she had prided herself on being the one who never needed anyone else. Her team, the family business, her parents' legacy—they were all counting on her to keep it together. Asking for help was a foreign concept, a vulnerability she refused to show, even when it would have been easier to lean on someone. She had convinced herself that she could handle everything on her own, and that gave her team and everyone who counted on her hope and confidence to pull through another day. But right now, as Jackson's gaze softened and his words held no judgment, only concern, the armor she'd spent years building started to crack.

Finally, Daisy let her walls down and the tears began to flow. They weren't just a sign of her exhaustion or frustration—they were an admission of something she had spent so long denying: that she couldn't do it all by herself. There were moments in life when even the strongest pillars needed support. For the first time in a long while, Daisy allowed herself to soften. She needed him, not just as a lover, but as the support she had long refused to ask for.

"Just catch me if I'm falling," she whispered, her voice trembling as she let the last of her defenses fade away.

Jackson held Daisy's gaze, his own eyes reflecting a mix of determination and tenderness. He pulled her into his arms, holding her close as she let out all the feelings she had been keeping bottled up for so long.

After a while, her emotions spent, Daisy nestled into Jackson's chest, feeling the steady rhythm of his heartbeat against her cheek. At that moment, she felt a sense of peace wash over her. His touch was a balm to her wounded spirit, a reminder that she wasn't facing the turmoil alone.

"You'll never have to face anything alone, Daisy," Jackson murmured as if he could read her mind. "I've got you, always."

The warmth of his body wrapped around her. Everything else faded away as they sat there in each other's arms, breathing in sync. In that moment, time seemed to stand still as they clung to each other, finding solace in the familiarity of each other's presence.

Daisy sighed and leaned back slightly to look into Jackson's eyes, her own eyes filled with a mix of gratitude and love.

"You know, Jackson, I was raised to be independent," she whispered, her voice barely above a breath. "I've always been able to take care of myself. But… when I'm with you, I… Well, I never thought I'd need someone like I need you. You give me light in the darkness, Jackson "

Jackson held Daisy's hand tighter. She could see that her vulnerability and honesty touched him deeply. His voice was steady and sincere. "Daisy, when we were apart, all I could think about was race day. Not just because I wanted to win, but because it was the only chance I had to see you. Watching your hair fall down your back, hearing you laugh at a meet and greet with the fans… and if I was lucky, getting a whiff of your perfume right after you'd been in the media room before me. Those moments kept me going, hoping you'd find your way back to me."

Daisy felt a surge of warmth in her chest, a mixture of elation and gratitude at Jackson's words.

"What I'm trying to say is…" Jackson took a deep breath, his stare unwavering. "You've taken the wheel of my heart, Ms. Kray, and I'm fully in your control. I'm all yours—through the high-speed turns and straightaways, through every pit stop and victory lap. My body, my soul, everything is in your hands. I love you."

Overwhelmed by the intensity of Jackson's love and devotion, Daisy wrapped her arms around him, melting into a kiss. She felt the warmth of Jackson's hand around hers, the tips of his fingers brushing against her skin. His breath warm and inviting, as he leaned in closer. When their lips finally met, everything else faded away, leaving only the charged connection between them.

Jackson eventually sat up and coaxed Daisy's arms around his neck. With care, he scooped her up, cradling her close. Chief nudged gently against them as if offering his silent support. Without a word, Jackson carried her out of the barn, Daisy's head resting against his shoulder, the night air cool and fresh around them.

Chapter 23

Daisy lay snug against Jackson's bare chest as he held her in his bed, stroking her hair tenderly, his fingers combing through the familiar waves as he pressed gentle kisses to her head. For a moment, everything else faded away. The chaos, the threats, the fear—it all felt distant as he cradled her close.

He marveled at how this woman had burrowed so deeply into his heart. He had never felt this way about anyone before. She was fierce, independent, and could handle herself better than anyone he knew. But, damn, she felt fragile in his arms. The way she had opened up to him—telling him she needed him, that he gave her light in the darkness—made his heart swell with an intensity he hadn't expected. Almost losing her had shaken him to his core, but it had also strangely grounded him, making him realize he couldn't imagine his life without her.

Jackson thought about their future, knowing that being competitors on the track could complicate things, but at that moment, none of that mattered. What mattered was that she was here, safe, and she was his. He traced a finger along the curve of her back, listening to the soft rhythm of her breathing, relieved that she was finally getting some rest. Sleep eluded her lately and seeing her so peaceful now filled him with a sense of calm.

Just as he felt his own eyes start to close, the vibration of his phone shattered the tranquility. He frowned, his muscles tensing immediately. The phone buzzed again, lighting up on the nightstand. He contemplated ignoring it, not wanting to disturb Daisy's sleep, but something about the late hour made him reach for it.

Gently, he shifted, pulling his arm from under Daisy as she rolled onto her side. He reached over for the phone, careful not to make a sound. When he glanced at the screen, it read "Unknown Number."

The call stopped, but a second later, a text notification appeared. Jackson's jaw clenched as he opened the message. His heart lurched at the image that filled the screen—Daisy, struggling in Lumen's self-driving car, the seatbelts locked tight across her chest and deepening into her wound, a look of panic on her face.

Jackson's stomach dropped. He carefully maneuvered himself out of bed, trying not to disturb Daisy. His adrenaline rushed as he crossed the room to the master bathroom. Closing the door softly behind him, he tried to catch his breath. The phone buzzed again, the unknown number flashing once more.

Without hesitation, he answered, his voice low and deadly. "Who the hell is this?"

A familiar voice, slick and taunting, oozed through the speaker. "Hi, Jackson. Lumen Ross calling. It's been years, hasn't it? Did you get my text?"

Jackson's fist clenched around the phone, his anger flaring to a boiling point. "You son of a bitch!" His voice was barely a whisper, but the fury behind it was palpable.

Lumen laughed softly, a sound that made Jackson's blood run cold. "Just wanted to ask how it felt watching Daisy forced into my car and then driven away. You were right there, and she slipped through your fingers. I have to admit, I expected more from you."

Jackson's heart raced, the image of Daisy in that car flashing through his mind again. He had saved her, but Lumen's words pressed hard on him. He gritted his teeth, his breath coming in heavy. "I swear to God if you even think about coming near her again—"

Lumen cut him off with a sneer. "Oh, don't be so dramatic. You know, I always thought I'd be a better match for Daisy. After all, I understand her in ways you never could.

You're just the farm boy playing house with a woman far out of your league. I would've given her the world."

Jackson's grip on the phone tightened, his knuckles white. "You're delusional."

Lumen laughed again, the sound grating on Jackson's nerves. "Mark my words, Jackson—you, Roger, and the feds won't be able to protect Team Kray forever. Daisy, Kelli, Morgan… I'll get to each of them, one way or another."

Jackson's rage erupted, his voice shaking with fury. "If you try to touch any of them, I will end you, Lumen. I swear on my life—I'll make sure you never get another chance."

There was a pause, and then Lumen's voice came through, amused and cold. "Tell Daisy I look forward to seeing her again very soon but I have an errand to run first. Have a good night, Jackson."

The call ended with a sharp click, and Jackson stood there, his chest heaving with rage. He stared at the phone in his hand, the image of Daisy's terrified face still burned into his mind. Without wasting another second, he dialed Agent Turner.

She answered on the first ring. "Jackson, I …"

"Lumen called me," Jackson interrupted, his voice thick with tension. "He sent me a picture of Daisy in that damn car."

"We know. We're tracking your phone and we're on our way over," Agent Turner replied, her voice calm but firm. "Stay put. We've notified agents outside your house and the agents with Morgan are on alert."

Jackson hung up, his blood still boiling as he leaned against the bathroom sink. He glanced at the closed door, knowing Daisy was still asleep on the other side. She didn't need to know about this right now. Not yet.

Taking a deep breath, Jackson stepped out of the bathroom and quietly made his way down the hallway to his den. The darkness of the house felt suffocating, but his mind was laser-focused. He reached the locked cabinet in the corner of the room, his fingers trembling slightly as he typed in the code.

The door clicked open, revealing seven shotguns lined up neatly inside. He pulled one out, his movements methodical as he loaded it, checking each shell with precision. The feel of the gun in his hands was steadying, a reminder that he wouldn't let anyone hurt the people he loved.

He sat down in the chair, the shotgun resting across his lap, his jaw set in determination. "You just try to come back here, you son of a bitch," he muttered under his breath, his voice low and dangerous.

Jackson knew this wasn't over. But whatever was coming, he would be ready.

Chapter 24

Kelli glanced up from her tablet and peered out the living room window of her remote Nashville rental home, observing the two FBI agents stationed just outside. She watched as one agent, Ramirez, adjusted his stance, scanning the area with focused eyes that rarely lingered in one place for long. His partner, Baker, kept a close watch on the house itself, his gaze steady as he checked each entry point, the sweep of his flashlight briefly illuminating the darkened windows. To keep lines of communication open, a compact FBI radio went with Kelli wherever she went so she could listen in on everything observed in and out of the house.

Tall pines and dense undergrowth bordered the property, their shadows creeping like silent figures in the dim moonlight. The house sat alone at the end of a winding dirt road, with no neighbors in sight. The isolation was palpable, the quiet broken only by an occasional gust of wind rustling the branches or the faint crunch under an agent's boot. Kelli shivered, feeling the vastness of the night pressing in, making her acutely aware of how alone they were out here.

As she turned her gaze back to a racing video on her tablet, Kelli felt a nagging sense of unease growing. It wasn't that anything seemed outright wrong—it was the absence of normalcy, the strained quiet that left her hyper-alert. The last few weeks had pushed her to the edge, but she tried to keep her fear in check. She didn't want her parents to see how rattled she was; they were already dealing with enough. Kelli had convinced them to go out earlier, to get away from the tension in the house, and now that they were asleep, she felt the responsibility to hold it together even more. She forced herself to breathe, to stay calm, but the pit in her stomach continued to grow.

Daisy flickered into Kelli's mind, grounding her. As a mentor and close friend, Daisy had always been her anchor, the one who made her feel like she could face anything. Daisy's resilience was something Kelli admired, and thinking of her now reminded Kelli that she needed to be strong too. She couldn't afford to fall apart, not when the stakes were so high.

The faint sound of a car engine interrupted Kelli's thoughts. Her heartbeat accelerated and her fingers froze over the tablet as she strained to listen. The hum grew louder, unsettling in the quiet night. She moved toward the window and saw the car gliding silently up the driveway into the bright security lights, its tinted windows black as ink. The agents cautiously stepped forward, their expressions wary as they watched the vehicle come to a halt in front of the house.

"Unidentified vehicle approaching," Ramirez's voice crackled over her radio, calm but filled with urgency. Kelli's breath caught in her throat as she registered the tension in his tone. She watched as the agents observed the car, their postures rigid, hands hovering near their weapons. Her sense of unease accelerated as Baker raised a scanner to examine the vehicle, his brow furrowing as he studied the readout. Something was very wrong.

Kelli took a shaky breath, her mind grappling with the implications. Why was there no driver? And why did this car feel so... sinister? She could barely pull her eyes away from the eerie, unmoving vehicle, and felt a cold wave of dread wash over her.

Suddenly, Baker's voice cut through the silence, reaching into the house with a note of urgency that made Kelli's skin prickle. "Kelli, we need you and your parents out now. This isn't a drill!"

His words snapped her into action, her body moving before her mind could fully catch up. She jumped off the couch and bolted down the hallway, throwing open the door to her parents' room.

"Mom, Dad, wake up! Something's wrong, and we have to leave. Now," she whispered, trying to keep the panic from her voice.

Her mother sat up, eyes wide in confusion, while her father rubbed his face, trying to shake off the sleep. "What's happening?" he asked, swinging his legs off the bed.

"No time—just come on!" Kelli insisted, tugging at her mother's hand and leading them quickly down the hall. Her heart pounded with urgency, each step amplifying the terror clawing at her.

Outside, Ramirez and Baker moved cautiously back from the car, keeping a safe distance as Baker confirmed their fears. "It's a bomb," he said, his voice grim. "Timer's active. We need to move fast."

Kelli's pulse hammered as the agents hustled her and her parents down the steps to the backyard. Everything felt surreal like she was watching herself from a distance. The sound of her shoes scuffing the ground, the solid grip of Ramirez's hand guiding her forward, the panicked breaths of her mother beside her—all of it felt sharper, more immediate as if her senses were on overdrive. She held tight to her mother's hand, feeling the fear radiating from her parents, the terror mirrored in their eyes.

As they neared the edge of the property, Kelli's gaze flicked back to the house. Her heart twisted as she realized that everything they had sought refuge in—the safety, the quiet moments they tried to salvage—was about to be blown apart.

"Down!" Ramirez shouted, pushing them toward a cluster of trees as the explosive timer neared its end. The family threw themselves to the ground, pressing against the earth as they covered their heads.

In that split second, a thunderous explosion ripped through the air, shaking the ground beneath them. The blast lit up the night sky, casting an eerie glow over the woods as a searing wave of heat washed over them. Kelli closed her eyes, feeling the rush of hot air graze her back, the distant roar fading into ringing silence. She dared to look up, her vision blurred by the brightness, and embers swirled in the air, the house engulfed in flames.

Kelli's ears rang with a deafening buzz, the sound of the explosion still echoing in her head. Her body tingled with adrenaline, every nerve on edge as she slowly pushed herself up from the ground, her eyes wide as she took in the destruction before her. Her parents scrambled to their feet beside her, coughing from the smoke that hung heavy in the air. Kelli winced at the sight of her parents' stunned expressions, a mix of fear and disbelief on their faces.

As the initial shock of the blast settled, Kelli's mind struggled to process the sight of their former refuge now on fire. Her mother sobbed quietly beside her, clutching her father's arm, her father's face froze in stunned silence. Kelli's hands shook, trembling from the shock over how close they had come to disaster.

"Are you okay?" Ramirez asked, his gaze searching her face as he took stock of their condition.

Kelli nodded, though the truth was far more complicated. She felt shattered, the memory of her attack pressing on her chest, but somewhere beneath the fear and shock was a simmering fire.

Ramirez called Agent Turner with an update.

"We copy, ma'am," Ramirez said into the phone. "Kelli, once you and your parents have been examined by paramedics we've been ordered to immediately take you to the Wyatt Ranch."

As help began to arrive on the scene, Kelli stood still, watching from afar the firefighters trying to stop the spread of the explosion's blaze. In an instant, she realized this nightmare was far from over.

Chapter 25

The evening air thickened with impending rain, a humid tension that seemed to seep into every corner of the Wyatt ranch. Daisy paced near the window, her eyes darting from the dirt road to the driveway, waiting. Her heart thumped wildly, each beat hammering out her silent hope: *Let Kelli be okay. Please, let her be okay.*

As headlights appeared on the horizon, her heartbeat quickened, her hands clenched in suspense. When the car door opened and Kelli stepped out, Daisy exhaled a breath she hadn't realized she'd been holding. The relief was so strong, it left her dizzy. She rushed forward, closing the distance between them, her hand reaching out instinctively. Kelli's arms were barely open before Daisy pulled her into an embrace, clinging tightly.

"I couldn't bear losing you, kid," Daisy murmured, her voice thick with emotion. She felt Kelli's smaller frame shake as they held each other. Kelli was safe. For now.

Kelli's parents exchanged grateful nods with Jackson and Papa Joe, as they followed them inside. The agents filled the room with their dark uniforms and equipment, their expressions grim and businesslike. The ranch, a place that had always represented comfort and family to Daisy, felt like a war room. Firearms rested within easy reach, and urgent, whispered conversations filled the air.

Daisy could see the toll of long hours on Agent Turner's face, deep lines cutting across her brow as she reviewed notes on her tablet. Despite her fatigue, Agent Turner's gaze remained sharp and focused as she briefed the team. She introduced the newest addition to their ranks, FBI Cyber Special Agent Ethan Fields.

"Agent Fields isn't just one of our top cyber specialists in AI and tech," she said. "He's also a huge stock car racing fan."

Agent Fields adjusted his glasses, his eyes flickering nervously toward Kelli. Daisy noticed the flush creeping up his neck, and despite the tension in the room, a small, almost amused smile tugged at her lips. It was one of those fleeting, absurd moments that, somehow, managed to bring a touch of humanity into the chaos.

Agent Turner cleared her throat, drawing everyone's attention back.

"We've been able to confirm through tech analysis that Lumen Ross is operating from within the Nashville area. Based on vehicle signals from the car we intercepted and the explosive vehicle at Kelli's rental home, we know he's close. We've also gathered data from Jackson's recent phone call with him—Lumen was indeed in Nashville at the time."

Jackson moved closer, his arm wrapping protectively around Daisy's shoulders. She leaned into him, comforted by his touch, but her mind spun with fear and frustration. No matter how much security they had around them, Lumen seemed one step ahead.

Agent Fields, still fidgeting with his tablet, spoke up. "From the data we've collected, there are two other driverless vehicles, similar in design and frequency, that haven't been activated yet. Lumen still has resources at his disposal."

His eyes widened slightly as he met Daisy's gaze. "We believe he could deploy them soon, though it's unclear if he would target the ranch or use them elsewhere to throw us off."

The knowledge weighed heavily on Daisy, and she forced herself to focus. As Fields explained the specifics, Daisy's thoughts drifted. She looked around at everyone gathered here, risking themselves because of her and the revenge Lumen was seeking.

And yet, as she looked at Agent Turner's weary but determined face, she felt a realization settle over her. No one here could draw Lumen out but her. *They're protecting me from him,* she thought, *but the only way to end this is to put myself in his line of sight.*

Daisy shook her head slightly as if to clear the thought away. But she couldn't escape the feeling that this was the only solution, the one no one wanted to say aloud. She caught Agent Turner glancing at her, a sharp and thoughtful look that made Daisy think the agent knew it too, even if she couldn't say it.

Meanwhile, Agent Turner's phone buzzed insistently on the table beside her, but she let it ring, focused on the debrief. Finally, she sighed, exchanging a look with Agent Fields.

"We have another potential lead," she said. "Lucy Ross, Lumen's younger sister, is being brought stateside from the Cayman Islands as we speak. We suspect Lumen contacted her in the weeks leading up to the Tennessee 400. She may know more about Lumen's movements."

Daisy crossed her arms, her gaze skeptical. "Agent Turner, Lucy, and Lumen were never close. From what I know, Lucy hated racing and stayed out of everything Lumen cared about."

Agent Turner nodded, though her expression remained firm. "That may be, but it's the best lead we have. Based on calls logged in the recovered vehicle, Lumen reached out to Lucy several times. It's possible he confided something, or maybe Lucy has insight that could give us a way to draw Lumen out. We're also hoping Lumen will respond to us if we throw Lucy into the mix."

Papa Joe looked puzzled. "What do you mean by Lumen responding to you? Do you know where to call him now?"

Agent Fields jumped in, eager to share his findings. "Now that Lumen made contact with Mr. Wyatt's phone, we were able to track the unknown number to an unregistered burner phone—a private number that we believe Lumen is using as a personal line."

Daisy caught Agent Turner looking at her with curiosity so she shifted her attention to the room. She saw her friends, her family, and now, her protectors. Jackson's arm remained a steady weight around her shoulders, and she knew he would do anything to shield her from the threat outside. Yet, the pang of guilt grew to a stab. A feeling that she might have to go against every attempt they created to keep her safe.

Agent Turner's phone buzzed again, louder this time, breaking the silence as everyone's conversations fell away. The agent finally picked it up, her face clouding as she listened. Daisy's heartbeat accelerated as the agent's pinched expression sent a chill through her.

At the same moment, Jackson's phone buzzed, and Daisy felt him tense. His eyes scanned the text, and he looked at Daisy, his face pale.

"Daisy," he said, voice low and tense. "Roger just texted. Morgan's been taken into surgery for an emergency C-section. The baby's in distress."

A shock of dread washed over Daisy, leaving her breathless. Her mind reeled, guilt gnawing at her. *If only I could have kept Lumen out of our lives, maybe Morgan wouldn't be in danger.*

Agent Turner's voice was grim as she hung up her call and carefully approached Daisy. "The FBI office just called—Charlotte Medical Center is being evacuated. A car parked in the garage exploded. They're containing the fire, but portions of the hospital are being cleared. Thus far it has not affected the surgery floor your sister is on right now."

The news struck Daisy like a punch. She wanted to get to Morgan, to be there for her sister. She knew that Lumen's reach extended even to Charlotte, and this attack was meant to shake her resolve.

Her fears, which simmered just below the surface since Kelli's attack, transformed into a blazing anger that overpowered her in her desire to protect her sister. She had spent enough time on the sidelines, recovering, being protected, and feeling doubt. At that moment, she knew it was time to take matters into her own hands. It was time to steal the lead from this maniac. To go full throttle. As Papa Joe told her in the meadow, to stop living under caution.

No one else can do this, Daisy thought. *This ends tonight.*

Chapter 26

The oppressive warmth clung to Agent Turner's skin as she stood inside the barn, her gaze fixed on Daisy. The evening grew heavy, a storm pushing in from the west, the distant rumble of thunder vibrating through the ground beneath her boots. Sweat trickled down her neck, the intensity of the moment almost suffocating her.

"I can't let you do this," Agent Turner insisted, her voice sharp and to the point. It wasn't a refusal—it was a plea, one that she wasn't sure she believed in herself.

Daisy's eyes never wavered, her expression resolute. She wasn't backing down. Agent Turner knew it wasn't just a plan—it was *the* plan. If it worked, it would be a game-changer, a way to end the terror once and for all. But the risks were massive. There was no going back.

"You're offering yourself up as live bait," the agent continued, the words sounding foreign on her tongue, like a decision she could never make herself. "You understand what that means, right?"

"Of course I do," Daisy replied. "But I'm the best shot you've got. If we wait for Lucy Ross to 'work her magic'—if she even can—this will go on for who knows how long. Lumen will keep attacking people I care about. I can't let that happen."

Agent Turner stood silent for a long moment, letting Daisy's words sink in. It wasn't just about ending the manhunt—it was about ending this nightmare, once and for all. But could she let Daisy walk into the fire? Could she allow it, knowing the price?

"I'm a sure thing," Daisy continued, her eyes hard, unwavering. "You don't have time for *maybe*."

Agent Turner didn't want to agree. She didn't want to put Daisy in harm's way. But there was no denying that Daisy was the key. Not Lucy. Not anyone else. If Lumen was going to come out of hiding, it had to be because of Daisy.

But there was more at stake than just Daisy's safety. If this went wrong, it could cost Agent Turner everything. Her career. Her conscience. Yet Daisy was right. The plan was brilliant. Dangerous, yes. But brilliant.

"I can't let you go rogue, Daisy," Agent Turner said, her voice tight. "You follow the plan. You don't act on your own. Understand?"

Daisy nodded. "Of course."

Agent Turner's eyebrow arched. Daisy had something up her sleeve. She was too compliant. There was more and the seasoned agent felt uneasy, but before she could respond, a voice cut through the tension in the barn, deep and familiar.

"I don't like this," Jackson said, his tone low, as his figure emerged from the shadows near the barn entrance. He was standing just a few feet away, arms crossed tightly over his chest. The muscles in his jaw flexed, his expression a mixture of frustration and concern.

Agent Turner's stomach twisted, recognizing the conflict playing out on Jackson's face. He'd been standing there, listening. She hadn't heard him approach, hadn't seen him come in. But he was there now, his protective force filling the space.

Jackson took a step forward, his eyes hard on Daisy. "You really think putting yourself in harm's way is the answer?" His voice strained. "I don't like the thought of you walking into this. You're practically handing Lumen everything he wants."

Agent Turner watched Jackson's every movement. She could see the love in his eyes, the way they softened whenever he looked at Daisy. It wasn't just lip service—it was as if this man *lived* for Daisy. It was clear how deeply he felt for Daisy. In a way, it touched her to see that kind of devotion. Yet she couldn't let herself get distracted by it. This was about the operation, not about feelings.

Daisy didn't flinch at Jackson's words. She stood tall, meeting his gaze with the same unshakable resolve she had shown Agent Turner. "You would do the same if you were in my shoes, Jackson. You know that."

Jackson opened his mouth to respond, but the words didn't come. Instead, his shoulders sagged slightly. "I'm not going to pretend like I wouldn't, but…" Jackson's voice softened slightly, his expression changing. He rubbed a hand across his face as if trying to reconcile the feelings swirling in him. "I just don't like it. I can't lose you, Daisy."

Daisy softened at that, her voice lowering but still firm. "I know. But I can't let this go on. Not when I know I'm the only one who can stop it."

For a moment, neither of them spoke. Agent Turner stood off to the side, watching the exchange, her heart thudding in her chest. Daisy was standing resolute in a way that was both terrifying and awe-inspiring. She was committed, and it was clear that nothing would change her mind.

Agent Turner let out a deep breath. She looked at Jackson then back at Daisy. It had been decided. There was no going back.

"If we do this," Agent Turner said, her voice tight, "I'm in control of the operation. You follow the plan, Daisy. No improvising. No taking unnecessary risks. You'll have two-way communication with me the entire time." She tried to keep the authority in her voice. "You understand?"

"Of course, Agent Turner. But you know as well as I do that even the best-laid plans need to adapt when things go wrong."

As Agent Turner looked at Daisy, she couldn't help but feel that Daisy was already aware of the danger and the uncertain outcome. But there were no other options left—they had run out of time.

"I'll take full responsibility," Daisy added, her voice quiet but determined. "But this *has* to happen."

As Agent Turner nodded, she reached into her bag and pulled out a small canister, holding it out to Daisy. "I can't give you a gun or any other weapon, but this…" She met Daisy's gaze with a hard, resolute look. "It's pepper spray. Highly potent. The kind you can't find in a store because there's no safety on it so be careful. Just in case you come face to face with Lumen, you've got something."

Daisy took the can and put it in her jacket pocket, smirking at Agent Turner. "Pepper spray. Yeah, that should do the trick against a guy who's been trying to kill me using autonomous vehicles."

Agent Turner met Daisy's gaze with a knowing look. "It's a hell of a lot better than nothing. Let's hope you won't even need it."

Chapter 27

Daisy read the nervousness in Jackson's eyes. The kind of nervousness that came with not knowing what to say or perhaps being afraid of saying the wrong thing. His jaw was tight, and the way his gaze flicked from her to the ground suggested he was trying to find the right words, carefully picking each one as if he were walking on fragile ground.

She felt genuinely touched by it. She knew he wasn't trying to control her or stop her—he was worried, not just about her safety, but about losing her. That realization hit her harder than anything else. Daisy wasn't sure how this would end, or if she would even make it back, but the fact that Jackson cared this much made her feel both loved and guilty.

She walked over to him slowly, letting her boots scrape against the dirt floor. She stood close enough now to feel the warmth radiating from his body, but he didn't turn to face her right away. His hands were buried in his pockets and his breath came out in short bursts, as if he were trying to calm himself before speaking.

"You're not going to stop me," Daisy said softly, her voice gentle but firm. She didn't want him to be upset, but she also knew she couldn't let him hold her back now. This was the only way to stop Lumen, and she couldn't let him—*or anyone*—deter her.

"I know," Jackson said, finally turning to face her. His voice was tight, barely above a whisper, as if he was struggling to get the words out. "I can't lose you, Daisy."

Daisy's heart twisted at the raw emotion in his voice. She reached for his hand, her fingers brushing over his skin, feeling the slight tremble in his grip. She held on to him for a moment, grounding herself in the comfort of his touch. He wasn't saying it outright, but his fear was palpable.

"I'm not going anywhere, Jackson," she said, her voice steady. "I'll be back. I promise."

He met her eyes. "You can't promise that, Daisy. This is dangerous. Lumen—he'll do anything to get to you."

"I know," she admitted quietly. "I know the risks. But I can't keep waiting, not while he's out there, hurting people. I need to do this. For all of us."

Daisy felt Jackson's grip tighten on her hand, his thumb brushing over her knuckles. "I don't want anything to happen to you," he whispered. His voice broke a little, and it tore at her heart.

"I'm coming back to you, Jackson," she said softly, her thumb grazing his jawline as she reached up to gently tilt his face toward hers. "I don't know how this will end, but I *will* come back. You have to trust me."

Daisy saw Jackson's eyes soften, as he exhaled a heavy sigh. He lifted his hand to her waist and pulled her gently toward him. For a moment, neither of them said anything.

Daisy gave him a soft smile, trying to lighten the tension. "Besides, the plan calls for you to be driving a mile behind me with the FBI. You won't be far, and you know how much you love the view from behind me."

Jackson's lips twitched into a half-smile, the familiar warmth of their teasing banter slipping through the cracks of his worry. "Damn right, I do," he muttered, his thumb brushing over her cheek with a tenderness that made her heart flutter.

Daisy smiled as she leaned in to kiss Jackson, a slow, lingering kiss that communicated everything she couldn't put into words. It was full of the promise of return, of the deep connection they shared, and of the hope that everything would be okay. He deepened the kiss, pulling her closer, his arms wrapped around her as if he never wanted to let go.

When they pulled apart, both breathless, she rested her forehead against his, her hands still resting on his chest.

Jackson kissed her forehead softly, his lips brushing against her skin. "Please, come back to me."

"I will," Daisy promised. She stepped back, giving him one last smile before turning toward the door. Her heart was heavy, but her resolve was unshakable. The time for waiting was over. It was time to face Lumen.

With a final glance at Jackson, Daisy pushed open the barn door and stepped into the night. The storm was still looming in the distance, the rumble of thunder a reminder that things were about to get much more intense. But Daisy was ready. She had to be.

Chapter 28

The high-pitched ring of the burner phone that Lumen used to call Jackson pierced loudly, hijacking Lumen's attention. It wasn't completely unexpected—he'd anticipated it. But the urgency of it caught him off guard for a moment. *The FBI hackers are faster than I thought.*

Lumen answered as he took a seat in his car. "This is Lumen Ross. I assume this is the FBI?"

The voice that came through the line was not what he expected.

"No," she said, her voice sharp and full of venom. "It's Daisy Kray."

Lumen's body stiffened. He hadn't expected to hear from her, especially not now. He quickly recovered, his lips curling into a predatory grin as he met the gaze of his reflection looking into the car's rearview mirror.

"Well, Daisy," he purred, his tone now smooth and mocking, "how nice of you to check-in. I can't wait to see you soon."

Her voice cut through to Lumen, steady but cold. "Lumen cut the Bond villain crap. You're nothing but a coward!"

Lumen was speechless. It took a moment before he could respond. "What did you just say to me?"

Daisy continued. "You heard me. You sent a dying race car driver to do your dirty work, and then set him up to try to kill me in a race? You manipulate a ranch wrangler to get to me and to top it off, you use driverless cars because, you know, if your win-loss record in stock car racing taught you anything, it's that you can't drive worth shit."

Lumen's blood boiled, enflamed by the voice on the other side of the line. "You bitch!"

Daisy's voice did not back down. "Bitch? Is that the best you can do? I guess I would expect that from a washed-up driver who has to hide behind AI and a bunch of toys because he knows deep down inside he can't win on his own. Not on a race track, not in a fight, and not in life."

Lumen's pulse quickened, his fingers tightening around the phone. His chest tightened with both shock and rage. He hadn't expected this, but the insult, the challenge, only fueled his anger. The audacity of her to speak to him like that, to belittle him, made something dark churn within him.

This isn't right.

For the first time, he felt something shift inside—doubt, maybe? No, that wasn't it. It was fury. Real, gut-deep fury. He was supposed to be the one in control.

His mind whirled. *I'll make her pay for this. She'll regret underestimating me.*

"Daisy, you have no idea what I am capable of. I'll take everything from you—everything that means anything—and you'll be begging me for mercy before the end!"

Daisy responded to him without hesitation. "Then come get me, Red Devil. But you'll have to catch me first."

He leaned back in the car seat, his eyes narrowing, plotting his next move. Silence hung between them as he considered his words carefully. The thrill of the hunt coursed through him, but there was something more now—something deeper.

"Your confidence will be your downfall, Daisy," he hissed, his voice dropping low, dangerous. "I suggest you kiss your boyfriend long and hard because he's never going to see you again."

Another long silence followed before Daisy's voice came through the line, calm and unwavering. "I suggest you take a last drag of your cigar long and hard because they don't have those where you're going. I'll be in Mud Valley."

The words hung in the air. Mud Valley—an old dirt race track just south of Nashville that was the bane of his existence. His blood ran cold for just a moment. She knew. She *knew*. And that made the challenge even more infuriating.

The *audacity* of her to toy with him like this. She didn't understand the consequences of pushing him so far. But she would feel it soon enough.

He wanted to curse, to lash out, but instead, he pressed the button to end the call, anger bubbling just beneath the surface.

Lumen leaned back in the seat, his fists clenching. His breath came faster now, as though Daisy's words were still echoing in his ears.

For the first time, the thrill of the hunt felt different—this wasn't just about winning anymore. It was about *dominating* her, making her bend to his will. Making her regret everything she'd said.

His pulse quickened, the need to break her settling into his bones. He wasn't finished yet. *Not by a long shot.*

Lumen's mind was already racing, plotting, calculating. His lips curled into a sinister grin as he remembered his trump card.

All he needed was for her to bring the Mustang GT 500. That would be the final piece. And then… it would be game over for Daisy Kray.

Chapter 29

The rain hammered against the windshield in bursts as Daisy's Mustang GT500 roared down the narrow country road. The world around her was bathed in darkness, the night still deep with only a few hours until the first rays of sunlight broke the horizon. A storm was coming, but for the moment, Daisy was completely in control.

Her hands gripped the steering wheel, fingers flexing over the leather as if a part of her, seamlessly connected to very move. The smooth hum of the engine beneath her, the familiar vibrations, the way the tires hugged the road—*she missed this*. The way the Mustang responded to each subtle shift in the gear, the precision of her movements as she downshifted, then eased into the curves. It exhilarated her. She hadn't realized she missed it so badly until this moment.

She slid the gear shift into place with practiced ease, the click of the lever almost a comfort as she accelerated. Her heartbeat synced with the power beneath her feet, and for the first time since the crash, she felt confident and at the top of her game.

The road ahead blurred as she pushed forward. Inside the car, Daisy's pulse quickened with every turn, every shift of the wheel.

Focus. No distractions.

She'd told herself a hundred times that she was doing the right thing—*the only thing*—but there was a moment, a split second when she wondered if she was crazy. What if this was the end? What if she *didn't* come back? But then the Mustang growled beneath her, and the doubt melted away.

There was no turning back now.

Suddenly, Agent Turner's voice crackled in her earpiece.

"Daisy, do you copy? This is Agent Turner."

The sudden intrusion startled her for a second, but she quickly adjusted the volume, her attention sharpening.

"Yes, copy, Agent Turner," she replied, her tone calm but alert.

"You're to proceed a mile ahead of everyone. Jackson is driving in the black SUV with me. Agent Fields is monitoring from the back seat," Agent Turner's voice came through, steady and authoritative. "I'll keep you updated. Just stay on course. Don't engage unless I say so."

Daisy acknowledged. "Copy that. Also, do you still think it's a good idea, letting Jackson drive?" Daisy couldn't help but tease.

A brief silence on the line before Agent Turner's voice sternly responded.

"Just don't make me regret this, Kray. This isn't the time for racing stunts."

Daisy chuckled softly, her eyes scanning the road ahead, feeling the rush of speed with every turn of the wheel. "I know, I know. But it's not like we have any other options, right?"

"Right. Now listen, Daisy," Agent Turner resumed, shifting into business mode again. "We've got agents already stationed around Mud Valley. We'll know if Lumen is there before you even arrive. Just get onto the track and make sure he sees you. Remember, you're not engaging unless we give you the signal."

Daisy tightened her grip on the wheel, her heart quickening at the thought of finally facing Lumen, but she didn't let it show. "Understood," she said, her voice steady but with an edge of excitement.

Agent Turner continued. "Once we have him in our sights, we'll take it from there. Do you copy, Daisy?"

Daisy didn't respond immediately, letting the words sink in. Daisy knew it wouldn't be that simple, and she wasn't about to pretend that it would be. The moment Lumen saw her, everything would change. Her gut signaled that she'd be on her own, no backup, no easy way out.

"I copy," Daisy finally said, her voice firm.

Just then, Agent Fields' voice interrupted. "Ms. Kray, I just have to say—Mud Valley? Brilliant."

Daisy barely had time to smile before Agent Turner's voice cut him off.

"Agent Fields, please enact radio silence unless you have something relevant."

"10-4, Ma'am, I copy that," Agent Fields responded quickly, and a smile tugged on Daisy's lips enjoying the banter between Tucker and Fields.

Turning her attention back to the road, Daisy thought about Mud Valley. The track itself was a cruel test of skill, with wide, sweeping turns that could easily turn into traps if a driver wasn't careful. The surface was notoriously tricky, shifting from slick mud to loosened gravel, making every lap a challenge. But it wasn't just the track that was brutal; it was the swamps surrounding it. Everything about Mud Valley screamed danger.

Drivers knew if they didn't respect the track, the track would humble them. It was a place where rookies were tested by seasoned veterans—harsh conditions, rough corners, and obstacles designed to break the spirit of anyone who wasn't up for it. It was rumored that if you could finish the course with a car still in one piece, you had earned your place among the pros.

Lumen Ross, however, had never finished it. His performance there was legendary—for all the wrong reasons.

The other drivers had even given him the nickname "Mud Devil," a reminder of his disastrous first attempt. It's the reason Daisy recommended the location to lure Lumen out of hiding. His ego couldn't resist taking the bait.

The faded sign for Mud Valley appeared in her headlights as it came into view, making her pulse quicken.

Agent Turner's voice broke through again. "Daisy, there's no sign of Lumen yet. Proceed with caution. Agents are standing by."

Daisy slowed as she turned onto the narrow, dark private drive leading to the track. The road was lined with thick trees, casting deep shadows that only added to the eerie quiet of the early morning. The only sound was the gentle hum of the Mustang's engine and the steady patter of the rain on the windshield.

"Daisy, two FBI cars are coming to your front and rear to escort you in," Agent Turner's voice came through again, smooth and measured. "You should see them in five... four...three...two..."

As the countdown reached one, the two FBI vehicles appeared in Daisy's rearview, flanking her Mustang. One car moved into position in front of her, its headlights cutting through the rain, while the other locked in behind her, creating a protective barrier.

Then, just as the FBI cars settled into position, a deafening *crash* ripped through the night. It was a sickening sound—metal on metal, an explosion of noise as one of the FBI cars violently shoved off its course. The front car slammed sideways, its tires screeching as it collided with a nearby tree. The sound of crumpling steel echoed in her ears, and the entire car twisted under the impact.

Before Daisy could react, a second, even more violent *bang* rocked the air—another self-driving car had barreled into the rear FBI vehicle. The back car spun out of control, and careened into the darkness, leaving a trail of sparks and debris. The crash was so violent, that the sound of shattering glass and bending metal reverberated through the rain-soaked night.

Daisy jerked her car to the side from the shockwave of the crash. For a moment, her steering felt out of control, but her hands tightened around the wheel, forcing the car to stay straight so she could make her way onto the Mud Valley track. Loud voices crackled through her earpiece, but she tuned them out, her focus narrowing.

As she entered the track, a piercing static emerged through the earpiece. The voice that followed made her blood run cold.

"Daisy, my apologies for having to rely on my driverless vehicles to get your posse out of the way. It will be you and me from now on. You better keep that engine running because I'm right behind you, ready to make my entrance."

Before Daisy could respond, Lumen's red sports car burst through the gate like a beast unleashed, tearing down the path toward her, the screech of its tires slicing through the air. Daisy slammed her foot on the gas, the Mustang roaring as she narrowly swerved to avoid him. The Mustang slid into a sharp turn, tires screeching, her car barely holding on as Lumen's car followed close behind. She could hear him, the predator getting closer with every second, and she *knew*—this was a fight for survival.

The screech of tires and the roar of Lumen's engine were all she could hear as the two cars tore around Mud Valley's track. The rain had turned the surface into a slick, unforgiving mess, but Daisy held her own, the Mustang responding to her every move. She slid through the corners with precision, feeling the thrill of the chase surge through her. Lumen was close—too close—and he wasn't backing off.

She glanced at her rearview mirror, catching a flash of red through the sheets of rain. He was on her tail, pushing harder than ever, trying to force her into a mistake. Daisy tightened her grip on the wheel, her knuckles turning white. The track was wide enough now for both of them, but the turns were tight, and the wet dirt only made things trickier. The storm was intensifying, rain pelting the cars in sheets, reducing visibility to almost nothing. Lightning cracked through the sky, briefly illuminating the track in a stark, blinding flash.

She could feel the Mustang beginning to lose traction in the heavy rain, but Daisy was prepared. She'd driven through worse, and tonight, she wasn't about to back down. The Mustang's engine purred, responding to each shift of the gears, and Daisy forced herself to stay focused. *Just keep moving.*

Lumen was inches away now, his headlights bearing down on her in her side mirror. He was trying to get alongside her, aiming for the inside line on the next corner, but Daisy knew better. She flicked the steering wheel left, cutting the turn just enough to force him wide.

"Not today, Lumen," she muttered, her heart pounding in her chest.

But as they rounded the bend, something inside her clicked. The opportunity was there. The track straightened out, the road ahead wide and clear.

With a sudden surge of power, Daisy slammed the pedal to the floor, the Mustang leaping forward with terrifying speed. The roar of the engine filled her ears as she blasted down the straightaway, pushing the car harder than she ever had before. She wasn't just racing against Lumen now—she was racing against time. The storm was closing in, and she knew the clock was ticking.

As they neared the end of the track, Daisy glanced to her left, where the fence line blurred in the rain. She swerved hard. The car fishtailed for a moment but regained its composure. She could see Lumen's headlights in the distance, his car close behind, and she could hear the radio crackling in her ear.

As Daisy slammed the Mustang's gearshift, she noticed Lumen wasn't following. His sports sedan had disappeared into the mist of the storm. She accelerated, feeling the surge beneath her hands as she navigated the slick road.

I'm not out of this yet, she reminded herself. She needed to stay sharp.

Then, just as she began to settle, Agent Turner's voice crackled in her ear. Her pulse quickened again.

"Daisy, this is Agent Turner. Daisy, do you copy?"

The familiar tone in Agent Turner's voice comforted her. There was something oddly reassuring about hearing Agent Turner's voice, even through the static, as if everything would be okay now. She quickly adjusted the volume on the earpiece. "Copy, Agent Turner," Daisy replied, her voice steady.

"Daisy, you need to drive outside the track. Follow the fence line until it ends, about a mile from the track. We've got Lumen surrounded, but you need to stay out of sight. Wait for further instructions. Do you copy?"

Relief surged through her chest. They had Lumen surrounded. Daisy nodded to herself as she eased the car through another turn. The lights of the Mustang flickered through the downpour, cutting through the darkness as she followed the path Agent Turner had directed her on.

There was no one behind her now. The area outside the track was deserted, only the occasional crack of thunder breaking the tense silence. She felt a slight discomfort.

This doesn't feel right.

Daisy pressed on, but the darkness outside the Mustang felt suffocating, the rain hammering against the windshield louder than the engine's rumble. It felt like the world was shrinking around her, the wet road barely visible in the headlights. Still, she kept her foot on the pedal, a quiet determination building. The Mustang was responding, gripping with every turn, but something inside her still gnawed at her.

"Agent Turner," Daisy said into the earpiece. "I'm not seeing anyone. Do you copy?"

Static responded.

The sudden silence in her ear tightened her stomach. Her unease deepened as the road grew quieter.

"Agent Turner, please come in," Daisy tried again, her voice laced with frustration.

Nothing. Just static. Her grip instinctively steadied the car through another sharp curve.

Just as she was about to call again, the voice came through—cutting through the static with startling clarity.

"Daisy, I repeat, this is Agent Turner. Proceed with caution. Agents are en route. You need to keep driving until you reach the end of the fence line. Do you copy?"

The words—utterly familiar, utterly authoritative—settled into her mind, and Daisy allowed herself a brief moment of confidence. *Agent Turner's voice. It's real.* She didn't feel alone anymore. She trusted the plan.

She continued, her hands moving with confidence as she navigated the pitch-black roads. *Just a little further, and everything will be fine.*

As thunder crashed, the space around her seemed to shrink. The lights from her Mustang illuminated nothing but the wet road ahead. She wasn't sure how far she had driven, but the terrain was changing. The road began to narrow, and then—out of nowhere—her headlights cut through the darkness to reveal a vast stretch of murky swamp ahead of her.

Daisy slammed on the brakes, the tires screeching as they fought against the slick surface.

No, no—this isn't right.

Daisy's car finally came to a halt. In front of her, the swamp extended into darkness, dead timber rising from the water like jagged teeth, small strips of forest surrounding the barren land. She had nowhere to go. She had reached the edge of the road. *No way out.*

Dread hit her in the chest like a sledgehammer.

She adjusted her earpiece. "Agent Turner, what the hell is this? Where are you?"

The sound crackled again, followed by silence. Daisy reached for her phone, fumbling as she tried to dial. But as the screen lit up, the signal was gone. Nothing. Not even a flicker of reception.

The air inside the car felt suffocating. Daisy's palms were slick on the wheel as she tried to calm her racing mind.

Suddenly, the unmistakable sound of an engine cut through the night air.

Lumen's car emerged from the shadows, its headlights cutting through the fog like a predator closing in.

Daisy barely had time to react before Lumen's vehicle slammed into the back of her Mustang, sending her forward to the very edge of the swamp with a sickening jolt. The sound of metal grinding against metal echoed in the rain-soaked night.

She whipped around to see him. His menacing grin as he pulled alongside her, his car now inches from hers. He was here. And he was playing his final hand.

Lumen's figure stepped out of his car and appeared by Daisy's side, his eyes gleaming with cruel satisfaction. He wiped the rain from Daisy's window with his sleeve and held his phone up, showing her the live feed of Morgan in a hospital bed—fragile, hooked to monitors, looking helpless. Dread coiled in Daisy's gut.

"Let me in, Daisy," Lumen screamed, his voice cutting through the rain. "Or you won't see your sister again."

She could feel the claustrophobia of the situation swallowing her whole. The car, the swamp, the storm—they were all the same now. Trapping her, pressing her into a corner where she couldn't breathe.

Still, Lumen smiled. She saw him stop momentarily and return to his car. He took out a crowbar and headed to the passenger door.

Lumen's crowbar hit the glass, each strike sending a tremor through Daisy's body, her heartbeat pounding in her ears. She couldn't focus on anything but the sound of metal on glass, his face just inches away from hers, that sickening grin stretching wider with each hit. The glass shattered with a final, bone-rattling crack, and the rain poured in through the jagged holes. She tried not to look at him but heard him scream.

"You wanted me out of the shadows. I'm here, Daisy!"

No way out.

Daisy drove the gear shift backward, trying to move the car in reverse to avoid the swamp in front of her. Her foot slammed on the gas, the engine roaring in response, but the car didn't move. It was stuck in the mud.

"Come on, come on!" she muttered through clenched teeth, her foot pressing harder against the gas pedal as she tried to will the car in reverse.

The tires spun wildly. She kept pushing, fighting, trying to escape, but the car wouldn't cooperate.

Lumen's laugh cut through the chaos.

"Still think I'm a coward? You can't escape, Daisy!"

Daisy's eyes widened in horror as she saw Lumen climb back into his car. His eyes locked on her, unblinking, as he accelerated the car with a violent jerk, tires spinning in the mud. Her stomach dropped as she realized his intention.

Lumen charged ahead, the engine's scream cutting through the air. Daisy's heart raced, her hands frozen on the steering wheel as she braced herself. Lumen's car crashed into her Mustang from the rear with a jolting collision, the force of the impact sending her spinning out of control.

In an instant, her car lifted off the ground, flipping through the air before plunging headfirst into the dark, murky waters of the swamp.

Everything went dark, the water pressing in from every direction.

Her mind raced, but every instinct told her to *get out*—to survive. Her heart hammered against her rib cage as she pushed herself against the door, but it wouldn't open. She fought for air, panic clawing at her throat. She felt herself slipping, the world around her spinning into oblivion.

Chapter 30

Agent Fields gripped his laptop tighter, his fingers flying over the keys as he tried to regain control. The rain pounded relentlessly on the windows, the vehicle hurrying with Jackson's frantic driving. Every swerve and turn threw Fields off balance, but he didn't dare ask Jackson to slow down.

The urgency in the car was suffocating. Everyone held their breath.

Agent Turner was sitting in the passenger seat, barking orders. "Fields, where the hell is Daisy? Why did we lose her?"

Agent Fields kept his eyes on the laptop, the glow of the screen illuminating his face. "I'm working on it, Agent Turner," he muttered, trying to ignore the frantic beat of his heart. "Just give me a few more seconds."

His fingers raced over the keyboard as he sifted through the code.

Damn it, Lumen.

Lumen was one step ahead again, jamming Agent Field's access at every turn. Then, as if by luck, the feed flickered. Agent Fields felt a rush of relief, and quickly scanned the data, eyes widening when he realized he'd gained access to Lumen's car.

Finally.

But as he listened to a playback he accessed from the car's communication log, Agent Fields' blood ran cold.

The voice that came through was Agent Turner's. But it wasn't right. It was too perfect, too controlled.

"Daisy, this is Agent Turner. You need to keep going straight. Take the left just ahead, and follow the fence line until it ends. We've got Lumen surrounded, but you need to stay out of sight until we can make a move. Do you copy, Daisy?"

Agent Fields' stomach turned. "No," he muttered under his breath, his hands shaking as he keyed in more commands.

This isn't right. It's not really her.

"Agent Turner, it's Lumen," Fields whispered, the reality hitting him. "He's using the technology to impersonate your voice. He sent Ms. Kray into a trap!"

Before he could speak further, Jackson slammed on the brakes, sending Agent Fields forward.

A lump formed in Agent Fields' throat, and for a moment, he thought he might lose his grip on the situation entirely.

Jackson's voice cut through the tense quiet, low, and furious.

"Where the hell is she, Fields?"

Agent Fields looked at him. Jackson's nostrils were flaring, and there was desperation in his eyes.

"I—I'm pulling the coordinates now, Mr. Wyatt," Fields stammered. "It looks like a swamp. Start heading east."

Jackson didn't hesitate. He slammed his foot down on the accelerator, pushing the car into the storm. Fields refocused on the laptop, trying to pull up the live feed from Lumen's car, desperate to locate Daisy.

Then the image appeared.

Agent Fields saw Daisy's Mustang upside down, sinking into the swamp. The headlights flickered, barely visible in the muddy water.

"Oh no," he whispered. The words left his lips before he could stop them.

"What's happening, Fields?" Jackson growled, his voice thick with frustration and fear. He wasn't slowing.

"I see it. I'm pulling up the live camera from Lumen's car," Fields said, barely able to breathe as he typed furiously. His hands shook as the feed came into full view.

There, standing knee-deep in the swamp, water dripping off him, was Lumen. Agent Fields could hear Lumen shouting down at the water and then saw him turn and walk back towards his car. Lumen's hair hung around his face, matted and dripping, and his eyes were wild with rage. As Lumen moved closer to his car, he looked directly at the camera, a twisted grin spreading across his face. He opened the driver seat door and turned the camera to show his expression in the full frame.

"Very clever, Agent, whoever you are," Lumen purred, his voice dark with amusement. "Your hacking skills are commendable. I'm sure I'll be seeing you soon. Oh, and please tell Jackson Wyatt that I have a surprise for him."

Before Fields could respond, the screen went dark, cutting off Lumen's sadistic leer.

"Fields…" Agent Turner's voice broke through, her tone a mixture of disbelief and anger. "How far are we?!"

"Under a mile, ma'am," Fields responded sounding anxious and dejected.

Agent Fields heard Agent Turner calling in for backup and Jackson pleading for Daisy's safety under his breath. For the first time in his FBI career, Fields felt helpless. Lumen had them all right where he wanted them. Worse, it felt like they had already run out of time.

Chapter 31

The engine roared in Jackson's ears as he slammed his foot down on the accelerator, driving the car forward through the rain-soaked dirt road. The world outside blurred, just flashes of shadow and darkness. Turner and Fields were tense in the car, but Jackson barely registered their presence. His mind was consumed with the thought of one thing only—Daisy.

He barely noticed the trees thickening along the road, the distant sound of the storm rumbling overhead. He just needed to get to her, needed to know she was okay. But the closer they got, the more uncertainty he felt. What if he was too late?

The car skidded to a halt as they reached the edge of the swamp. Jackson didn't wait for anyone else. The second the tires stopped rolling, he threw open the door and sprinted into the storm, his boots slapping against the wet ground as he ran toward the sinking Mustang.

The rest of the team were right behind him, but Jackson didn't look back. He only had eyes for the wrecked Mustang in the swamp.

Daisy. Daisy. Daisy.

Every footstep was a prayer for her safety. As he reached the edge of the swamp, he could see the broken remains of her car, but no sign of her yet. A scream rose in his chest, threatening to burst through, but before he could move, a shadow leaped from the woods.

Lumen.

Jackson barely had time to react before Lumen tackled him from the side, knocking him off balance and into the mud. A sharp pain shot up his back. He barely registered it before Lumen's fist came down hard, slamming into his ribs.

Jackson grunted. He swung his arm, catching Lumen across the jaw with a brutal punch, but Lumen barely staggered. Jackson had to give it to him—the bastard had stamina, lots of it. Jackson's fists kept flying, pounding Lumen's face, his stomach, his chest. Every strike was fueled by one thing: rage.

He couldn't stop. He couldn't let Lumen win.

Suddenly, Jackson heard Lumen try to speak. Blood in his mouth made it hard to get the words out. "Hey Jackson, didn't you think it was kind of easy getting Daisy's Mustang back?"

Jackson froze. A cold wave washed over him, the fight dying in his veins. He stared at Lumen, unsure what the hell he meant.

"Oh, Jackson. You really should be more careful about who you do business with."

Jackson scrambled to figure out how Lumen knew about him buying Daisy's old car back.

"Do I have to spell it out for you, Jackson?" Lumen teased. "I was the anonymous high bidder for Daisy's car at the auction. I knew it would be useful someday."

Jackson's mind spun, trying to process what Lumen was saying. "You were the one who sold it back to me."

Lumen grinned. "Sure was, and damn was it useful! Before it shipped to your place, I added a little surprise."

Jackson watched Lumen reach into his pocket and pull out a tiny remote control. "A new gear shifter with a very special feature. A little explosive hidden inside."

"You're a monster," Jackson muttered, looking at Lumen in horror.

"Ironic, isn't it?" Lumen asked. "Your desperate act of chivalry will ultimately kill her unless, of course, she's already dead."

Jackson's heart thundered in his chest as panic set in. He desperately wanted to run back to the swamp but didn't want to make a sudden move to provoke Lumen to set off the explosive.

Before he could react, Jackson heard Agent Turner and Agent Fields crashing through the trees, shouting orders as they sprinted toward them. But it was too late. Jackson's voice cut through the air, desperate.

"Turner! Stop! He has an explosive!"

The words were barely out of his mouth when Lumen's finger pressed the button. A violent *boom* ripped through the air, a shockwave that knocked Jackson and everyone else to the ground, sending the world spinning.

The explosion rocked the swamp, sending debris and water flying in all directions. Jackson could feel the intense heat from the blast, his ears ringing with the deafening sound. He struggled to push himself up from the ground, his vision blurry and disoriented.

"Daisy!" he shouted, struggling to get to his feet as he heard Agents Turner and Fields shouting into their radios for backup.

Jackson looked around frantically for any sign as the smoke cleared.

Lumen and Daisy were nowhere to be found.

Chapter 32

The cold, wet sting of swamp water registered against her skin. Daisy's eyes opened slowly, the world around her blurry, spinning. Her limbs felt heavy, sluggish with exhaustion. The tall swamp reeds pressed into her skin like sharp fingers, clinging to her as she fought to free herself. Her body ached, bruised, and battered from the crash, but it was the relentless exhaustion that nearly stopped her in her tracks. Every breath was a harsh reminder of the desperate struggle it took to escape the submerged car.

She remembered: *Sinking in the Mustang, the water rushing in, drowning her as she fought to stay afloat. The car that once held such wonderful memories became a death trap. Her seatbelt kept her in place, and with a panic-fueled jolt, she unbuckled the strap, pushing through the resistance of the sinking car. She had to get out. Reaching for the rear window, half-broken, she forced her body through the shattered glass, gasping as she made her way toward freedom. The cold water swallowed her whole, but she made it. She swam and hid among a cluster of swamp reeds keeping only her eyes and nose above water as she watched for any sign of Lumen.*

As she waited, she saw the explosion—an eruption of light and fire. Her beloved Mustang, now a twisted heap of metal, was engulfed by the violent blast.

She willed herself to focus on the present moment, but the images of the explosion flashed like a film reel in her mind. Just as her thoughts threatened to pull her under again, a sudden sound startled her. A frog, its slimy body leaping from the water with an unexpected splash, broke the trance. Daisy sucked in a sharp breath, her heart racing for a moment. Shaking her head, she forced the memory away and dragged herself from the water, grounding herself in the present. She couldn't allow herself to stay still. She *had* to move. Her chest burned as she struggled to pull herself up onto the safety of land. She heard distant voices but was unable to call out. Her lungs were raw, burning with each desperate gasp of air.

Her legs felt like rubber as she forced herself to keep going. Still, she had to keep moving. Get as far as she could from Lumen. She needed to escape.

As she walked on, her legs shaking, Daisy glanced up at the sky. The first traces of dawn painted the horizon with pale streaks of gray. She felt the wind shift, biting at her cold skin, and realized how badly her body ached. Her lungs continued to burn from the effort, but she had to push forward. She had to keep moving. There was no time to rest.

Suddenly, a voice pierced through the silence. It was not a distant sound, but rather one that seemed to come from right beside her.

Lumen's voice cut through the air, low and mocking, the sound of it making Daisy's pulse spike.

"I've been looking for you. Did you really think you could escape, Daisy?" His words were laced with amusement, a cruel smile barely visible in the dim light.

Lumen emerged from the shadows, his tall figure casting an imposing presence. Daisy froze, her heart leaping into her throat as the familiarity of the voice washed over her.

"You're not going anywhere."

His tall figure materialized from the shadows, casting an imposing presence. The hazy light from the rising sun revealed his dark silhouette against the backdrop of the swamp. As he moved closer, she could feel his heavy gaze on her, assessing, calculating. His footsteps were soft on the wet earth, yet every sound seemed amplified in her ears. Her breath quickened, panic seizing her insides.

Before she could react, Lumen stood next to her, with alarming speed. His body heat reached her before he even touched her, and the closeness made her stomach turn. His breath warmed against her skin, causing the hairs on the back of her neck to stand up. She tried to pull away, but Lumen was too fast. His hand shot out, catching her wrist with a vice-like grip. The force of it made her stumble, and he yanked her back against him. His touch was cold, too real, too dangerous.

"No one's going to save you now," he said, his voice low and venomous. He grabbed both her arms and pulled her from the swamp, dragging her away.

Desperately, Daisy dug her heels into the soft earth, hoping to slow his capture. She tried dragging her feet, fighting against his pull. Her legs were weak, but she pushed against him, the resistance nearly breaking her. But it only seemed to anger him more. His grip tightened, sending sharp waves of pain through her wrist.

Lumen's sinister laughter echoed in her ears as he pulled her toward the edge. "Don't worry, Daisy," he taunted, "This'll be over soon. You'll stop fighting soon enough. I'll make sure of that."

She let her body go limp, hoping he'd ease off his hold on her. She needed time to think. Her mind raced with strategies and plans, but she focused on slowing her breathing and calming her racing heart. She wanted to lull him into a false sense of security. Though outwardly submissive, inside she remained fiercely determined to escape and survive.

It worked. Lumen stopped. Daisy dropped to the ground and lay on her side with her face towards him, her eyes closed as if she had passed out. Through slit eyes, though, she desperately assessed her surroundings.

Lumen spoke, taunting her. "You know, Daisy, your family ruined my career. They got in the way of my future. Your father... he took everything from me. It's time for you to feel the way I felt."

His words cut deep, deeper than she wanted to admit. But they also fueled the fire in her. She wasn't going down like this. Not without a fight.

And then a moment of clarity. She remembered the pepper spray Agent Turner gave her.

When Lumen wasn't looking she slowly moved her hand over her zipped pocket and could feel the spray was still there. *If only he would get close enough.*

Lumen took a step forward and leaned over her. He placed his hands on her chin and lifted her head.

"Wake up, Daisy." He shook her head roughly, but she kept her eyes closed, forcing her body to remain still. His fingers tightened on her chin, pulling her face up to his. She could feel his breath, hot and foul against her skin. "Before you die, I want to mark this momentous occasion with one of my favorite cigars."

He took a cigar from his pocket, biting off the end and spitting it out. Daisy waited for him to pull out the lighter. And there it was.

Daisy felt a rush of adrenaline as she found her moment. Her hand hurried to her pocket, her fingers brushing the cold metal of the pepper spray can. "Didn't I tell you those things would kill you?" she growled.

In one swift motion, she pulled out the pepper spray, aiming the nozzle at the lighter's flame and pressing down on it as hard and fast as she could.

The world exploded in a blinding flash of light. Searing heat scorched her skin. She heard Lumen scream as fire engulfed his face, and his limbs flailed wildly in a desperate attempt to extinguish the flames. Realizing his fate, he lunged toward Daisy with a demonic glint in his eyes, determined to take her down with him into the fiery depths of hell.

Daisy staggered back, her heart pounding in her chest. She couldn't let him drag her down. Her legs felt like rubber as she scrambled backward, the ground slick beneath her. Lumen's burning form twisted in agony, his cries echoing in the night as he clawed at his face. Daisy's breath came in ragged gasps, her body on autopilot as she desperately searched for an escape.

With a final burst of adrenaline, she stumbled into the shadows, leaving behind the inferno she had ignited. Her pulse raced as she forced herself to keep moving, determined to survive.

She then heard a loud splash. She turned to see Lumen had jumped into the water of the swamp. Before she could process what she was seeing, she felt rapid, urgent footsteps approaching. Voices shouted incoherently, muffled by the sound of blood thumping in her head.

With every ounce of energy drained from her, Daisy crumpled to the ground, the weight of her body too much to bear. Her vision blurred, her limbs unresponsive, and just before the darkness closed in, a familiar voice broke through shouting her name.

Jackson...

The world tilted, the last of her strength slipping away as he reached her. She felt the warmth of his arms lifting her, but it only made the ground spin faster beneath her, a dizzying blur of fading consciousness.

Chapter 33

Jackson walked through the rows of headstones of the cemetery. Although it was a cloudy day in Charlotte, North Carolina, the heat was suffocating, yet it hardly touched him. His mind was elsewhere, pulled by the challenges of the last few months.

He gripped the small bundle in his hand—a dozen red gerbera daisies, their vibrant petals bright against the dark green leaves. His other hand clenched the small spare key to Daisy's Mustang.

His boots shuffled in the freshly mowed grass as he moved past row after row of weathered headstones. Each step felt like it was leading him into the past, into a place where he could no longer protect her. He thought of how his chest had tightened when he first found her after the explosion, the sense of loss choking him.

Then he reminded himself—against all odds Daisy had survived, which brought him back to the reason for his visit.

Just ahead was the grave of Daisy's parents—Carson James Kray and Linda Jane Kray, side by side, as if they had always belonged together.

A willow tree, an ancient sentinel above their graves, provided quiet solace. Its branches reached down, sweeping the ground as if trying to comfort him. He stopped a few feet away, staring at the two headstones.

Jackson bent down slowly, and set the flowers carefully on Mrs. Kray's headstone. His fingers lingered there, brushing against the cool stone.

"Mr. Kray, Mrs. Kray… I—" His voice caught, and he had to pause, swallowing the lump in his throat. The breeze rustled the leaves of the willow, filling the air with a whisper.

"Mr. Kray, I want to thank you," he said, his voice thick with emotion. "I know I said this to you before but I truly appreciate what you did for me. You gave me my first break when I started racing. You told me that if I wanted to make it, I had to trust the car. Trust the road. You were right. "

Jackson could feel his pulse accelerating.

"And, well… congratulations are also in order. Morgan and Roger's son, Colby. He's your first grandchild. You've gotta be proud. Colby Martin... now that's a race car driver's name if I ever heard one, though Morgan probably doesn't want to hear that," he added with a bittersweet smile.

Jackson let out a sigh, then turned his gaze to Carson Kray's headstone.

"I wanted to come here to talk to you about Daisy... I don't know where to begin. She's... she's everything to me, Mr. Kray, Mrs. Kray. The strongest woman I've ever known. The kind of person who takes everything the world throws at her and still keeps moving forward. I've seen her push herself harder than anyone, harder than I thought was possible. After everything Lumen did to her—what she went through in that swamp—I don't even know how she came back from that. I knew firsthand how fierce she was on the racetrack but to see how powerful she is off the track is amazing."

Jackson felt the memories of that night flooding him—the heat of the explosion, the terror of finding Daisy's Mustang upside down, finding her on the ground, then picking her up and carrying her away.

"I don't know how Lumen Ross is still alive. I hear his sister Lucy is keeping him alive in some ICU in Nashville... But if there's any justice left in this world, the Red Devil will burn in hell," Jackson muttered, his jaw clenching tight.

His hand hovered over the Mustang's key, still tightly gripped in his palm. The key was all that was left of Daisy's car. All that was left of that day.

"Mr. Kray, I'm sorry about the Mustang," Jackson continued, his voice softer now. "Thought I'd bring back at least the key. The rest of it, well, it's gone… down in the swamp." He winced as the words left his mouth. "But I'm doing my best to make sure Daisy doesn't lose anything else."

He paused, taking a deep breath.

"She pushed herself so damn hard from all of this, Mr. Kray. I don't know how she did it, but she came back. And when the FBI investigation was dragging on and the racing association was crawling through the muck, she kept her cool. Grace. Patience. You raised one hell of a woman."

He stood back from the grave and wiped his face, clearing the last of his thoughts.

"So there's a race this Sunday here in Charlotte," Jackson went on, his voice thick with emotion. "It's Daisy's first since the crash. They've got some new dates back on the racing schedule. A huge hometown welcome for her. She deserves it. She's earned it. But…" His voice trailed off, and his fingers tightened around the key in his hand. "I'm nervous, Mr. Kray. The stakes are higher now. But she'll be ready. She always is."

He hesitated before speaking again, his heart pounding in his chest.

"Which brings me to my visit. You see, I'm in love with her," he finally admitted, his voice breaking. "I don't know how this is going to work—the two of us being such competitors—but I've realized something over the last few months. She means more to me than anything. More than my own life. I know I've made my fair share of mistakes this year but I learned from them and learned a lot about myself along the way. I've learned how to be the man that Daisy not only wants but deserves. A man who proudly stands by her side without fear. I'm devoted to her. And I—I'm here, Mr. and Mrs. Kray, to ask you if I can have your blessing to ask Daisy to be my bride."

His heart pounded as he spoke the words he had been planning in his head for so long. He then pulled out of his pocket a small velvet box, revealing a two-carat square-cut diamond with a lustrous platinum band.

"I'm not sure when I'll propose. She's been through so much, and I want to make sure she's ready, that she's healed. But I want to spend the rest of my life with her. I want to be her partner in this crazy race of life, no matter where it leads us."

He closed the box with a snap and stared down at the headstones for a long moment.

"I know I might be asking for something a bit out of this world here but is there a way you can give me your blessing, Mr. and Mrs. Kray? Your approval means a lot to me."

Jackson gently removed two of the daisies from the bouquet, taking in the scent that reminded him of Daisy.

As Jackson stood there, holding the daisies in his hands, a sudden gust of wind swept through the cemetery, rustling the leaves of the willow tree. The breeze carried the faint scent of jasmine—something he hadn't smelled in years. It reminded him of the nights he had spent sitting under the stars with Daisy when everything felt like it was possible, when the world was a place of hope, not danger.

The sun, which had been hidden behind the thick clouds, broke through for the first time that day, casting a soft, golden light across the headstone. The rays fell on Mrs. Kray's grave, illuminating the name in a warm, ethereal glow. It was a sign, clear and undeniable as if the heavens themselves were reaching out to touch it.

The wind stirred again, but this time it wasn't a simple gust. The air around him swirled, shaking the daisies in his hand ever so slightly. Just then, two of the petals broke free, drifting softly through the air. They landed gently at Jackson's feet, brushing against his boots.

Jackson bent slowly, picking up the petals. As he did, he noticed a small movement out of the corner of his eye—a butterfly, its wings shimmering in the sunlight, fluttered near the gravestones. It landed lightly between them as if it had been drawn there by some unseen force. It stayed there, still and serene, a moment of peace in the middle of the chaos that had consumed him for months.

Jackson stood up, feeling the heat of the sun on his face. He wasn't sure how long he had been standing there, but he felt something shift inside of him. This wasn't just a random moment. The timing, the butterfly, the petals... it was a message. A blessing.

In a hoarse voice, he whispered, the petals still in his hand. "Thank you."

For the first time in what felt like an eternity, Jackson felt a deep sense of peace. The universe, or something more, had just given him the drive to move forward.

Chapter 34

Daisy stood in the quiet of her trailer. It was a sanctuary amid the chaotic energy of the race weekend. The soft sound of the crowd outside drifted through the walls, growing louder as the time for the race approached. She closed her eyes for a moment, trying to quiet the anxiety swirling in her gut.

It had been a whirlwind of activity from the moment she arrived at the track that morning. The hours had been packed with obligatory driver meetings, where the standard pre-race procedures were covered, but the lingering tension of the past few months was never far from her thoughts. Visits with sponsors, all carefully orchestrated, had to be brief and efficient—everyone eager to show their support, but no one daring to press too hard for answers regarding the ongoing investigations.

The FBI's presence remained heavy, as were the racing association's officials, both keeping a tight lid on anything related to the sabotage of the cars during the Tennessee 400. The air thickened with unspoken words, and the memory of Lumen Ross hung over every conversation. Daisy could feel the eyes of the world on her, knowing that questions would follow her every step.

The media handlers from the racing association were diligent, ensuring that only the race—and her performance—was discussed. Any attempt to veer off-topic, to touch on Lumen's attacks or the lingering questions about her stay at Jackson's ranch, was swiftly redirected. Daisy had answered the questions about Jackson with the same practiced response, a controlled smile never fully reaching her eyes, and she gracefully avoided any comment about Lumen or the FBI's investigation. She couldn't afford to get drawn into that today—not when everything rode on her performance.

Back in her trailer, Daisy finally had a moment to herself. The noise of race weekend slightly dulled as she took a moment to focus and breathe.

The Charlotte 600 was a grueling 600-mile test of strength and endurance. It felt fitting. This race was her test, too. Her strength had been worn down over the past few weeks, physically and mentally. The crash, the sabotage, the uncertainty about Lumen and the people who had hurt her—it all weighed on her, even if she tried to shove it aside. She fought through the pain of pushing her body back to a place where she could compete again, and now, she was facing the ultimate challenge: not just the race itself, but the quiet battle inside her mind—was she ready? Could she do this?

Daisy stared at her reflection in the small mirror across the room, looking at the person who had walked through fire and somehow came out stronger.

There she was. The woman who had survived that swamp, challenged and broken, was not the same woman who stood on the cusp of this race. She fought to get there—fought for her life, fought for her sanity, fought for her place in this world.

The racing world that had once been her refuge was now her battleground, but Daisy wasn't afraid. She had come through hell and back, and today, the finish line wasn't just about victory—it was about reclaiming everything that was taken from her.

She could do this. No, she *would* do this. She wasn't just racing for herself anymore. She was racing for everything she'd lost and everything she was about to gain. This was her moment. And nothing was going to stand in her way. The moment lingered like a quiet breath before a storm.

A knock on the door distracted her.

Daisy hesitated. She wasn't expecting anyone and she didn't want visitors.

She had enlisted Morgan and Roger to man the door, to ensure her downtime, so she was surprised by the interruption. This was supposed to be focusing time, for her to be "in the zone."

Daisy hesitated before answering as her phone vibrated with a text from Morgan.

"I think you should open your door."

Frowning, Daisy walked over to the trailer door.

"Coming," she called, her voice steadier than she felt.

As she opened the door, Jackson stepped through, his figure filling the small, cramped space. He moved with the ease of someone who belonged, as if the world outside hadn't already weighed him down. His presence was a force—strong, magnetic—and the air charged with electricity with every step he took toward her.

Daisy's eyes swept over him involuntarily. His racing suit clung to him in all the right places. The tight fabric molded to his broad shoulders, defining the man she had always admired, the man who had been by her side through it all. Every inch of him was built for speed and power. At that moment, the lines of his physique called to her.

It wasn't just the sight of him, though he looked every bit the competitor. No, it was more than that. It was the way he held himself, with a quiet intensity, as if everything around him, everything he did, was about something bigger than just winning a race. He didn't carry himself like a man racing for just victory—he was a man racing to hold onto something deeper, something real. And that something, Daisy realized, had worked its way into her heart.

She couldn't look away from him. He had become part of the landscape of her life without her even noticing, and now, here he was again, standing in front of her, silent and steady. His eyes locked with hers, and for a moment, nothing else seemed to matter.

"I wasn't sure if you were ready to see me but I couldn't stay away. I needed to see you." Jackson said softly, his voice low, tentative, almost like he was testing the waters.

Daisy opened her mouth to respond, but the words stuck in her throat. She didn't think she was ready for this. Not this moment, not this quiet intimacy before the race. But as she watched him, standing there, so confident, so grounded, she realized something she'd been avoiding. This wasn't just about the race. It wasn't even about what had happened between them. It was about what they meant to each other, whether they were competitors or not.

She swallowed hard, her voice barely a whisper. "You know my rule before a race. You shouldn't be here."

Daisy watched Jackson's lips twitch in a small, knowing smile. "I know," he said, his gaze softening, "but I couldn't let you go through this without one last piece of support. That I'm here, no matter what happens out there."

Daisy's chest tightened, a wave of gratitude and warmth flooded her. She hadn't expected this. Hadn't expected him to come to her before the race. Yet in Jackson's presence, everything she had been carrying, the doubts, the fear, the pressure of the race—suddenly felt lighter, as if he had just given her a small piece of something she didn't know she needed.

For a moment, neither of them said anything. The world outside was buzzing with the anticipation of the race, the sound of teams getting ready, the noise of the crowd—and yet, everything seemed to fade, leaving only the two of them in this space. His eyes softened as he stepped closer to her, and without thinking, Daisy reached out, touching his arm. The feeling was electric—familiar and comforting, yet so much more than that.

"I wasn't sure I wanted to see you before the race," she confessed, her voice quiet, but filled with emotion. "But now that you're here... it feels right."

Jackson's hand gently cupped hers, and Daisy felt his thumb brushing across her skin in a way that made her pulse quicken.

"You don't ever have to be alone, Daisy."

She looked at him. He was someone who had come to mean something to her, something she wasn't sure how to define, but something she couldn't deny. This, right here, was the truth of it.

As Jackson smiled, Daisy noticed his gaze twinkling with mischief. "Daisy, I do have one last request before I leave. My team and I would be honored to join your team in escorting you to your car. Would you be okay with that?"

Her pulse quickened, a mixture of gratitude, confusion, and warmth swirling in her. He hadn't just broken the rules; he had proven, once again, that his feelings for her went beyond the race, beyond the competition. In that moment, Daisy realized that both she and Jackson had discovered something vital—that their strength wasn't just in the battles they fought on the track but in the bond they had forged, a connection that had withstood every challenge they had faced. It was this understanding, this acceptance of each other, that made them unstoppable.

Daisy blinked, surprised, and then a laugh bubbled up from inside her. "Well, if you do, then the whole world will suspect we're being 'Jaisy' again."

Daisy noticed Jackson's grin widen, bringing a softness to his expression that made her heart flutter. He picked up her hand and pressed a soft kiss to her knuckles. "There's nothing to suspect. In my mind, Daisy, we never stopped."

Daisy's emotions swirled inside her as she absorbed his words. She didn't know how to respond, didn't know if words could even express everything she felt at that moment. But she leaned in, close to his ear, and whispered, "You know I'm still going to pass you on those final turns."

Jackson's laugh, deep and warm, captivated her as he playfully ran pieces of her hair between his thumb and fingers. "I wouldn't have it any other way, Daisy. Like you said, I never complain about the view when I'm behind you."

Chapter 35

Daisy's heart pounded as she stepped out of her trailer. She could feel the eyes of the crowd already on her, the stands packed with spectators eager to see her race again. She was not just a driver today—she was a symbol of resilience, of coming back from the impossible. And the pressure of it all pressed in on her. She shoved it aside.

She wasn't going to let it control her. Not now.

As Daisy made her way toward her car, Kelli joined her hand in hand. The crowd cheered, and the feeling of being a part of something bigger than herself washed over her. There was a standing ovation. The crowd called her name. She tried to focus on putting one foot in front of the other, but the emotion of it all swept through her, and tears stung her eyes. How could she not be moved? After everything—Lumen, the crash, the investigation—here she was, ready to race. She was going to do it for herself, for her team, and for the people who always believed in her.

As Daisy walked, drivers who had raced with her and against her stepped forward to shake her hand, offering congratulatory words or giving her a quick hug. A few of them stopped to wish her luck, and Daisy smiled and nodded. Although on the outside, she kindly exchanged pleasantries, inside, she was on fire. She was ready to prove to everyone—not just the racing community, but to herself—that she belonged here.

A familiar face broke through the crowd—Commissioner Antonio Rivera. Flanked by officials, he moved toward her, extending a hand, his expression full of admiration.

"Daisy, it's good to see you back in the car," Commissioner Rivera said, his voice thick with gratitude and respect. "You've done so much for this sport, and for all of us. It means a lot to have you here today."

Daisy smiled, grateful for the recognition. She took his hand and gave it a firm shake. "Thank you, Commissioner. Let's just focus on keeping the drivers in control of their vehicles today, okay?"

Commissioner Rivera's face cracked into a grin. "Oh, Daisy, let's not even joke about that! Have a good race."

The exchange left her smiling as she continued walking toward her car, joined by her team and Jackson's. The sound of cheering from the crowd, the flashes of cameras, and the movement of her family around her made the moment feel surreal. Jackson's team and hers formed a protective circle around her.

Daisy approached her car with Riley by her side. Pausing, her eyes looked for Jackson. He stood next to her, his hands on his hips, watching her, an unreadable look in his eyes. There was a moment—an intense, silent moment—where everything seemed to hold still, just for her.

He gently cupped her hand in his, pressing a tender kiss to her palm, a silent promise that spoke louder than any words could. The soft touch sent a jolt of warmth through her. She then watched him turn, heading toward his car with the rest of his team. She waived at Papa Joe, standing nearby before he followed Jackson.

Daisy's heart softened, watching him go. But before she could dwell on it too long, Morgan and Robert were at her side, with Baby Colby in Morgan's arms. The moment was full of love, and support—everything Daisy had fought for. She bent down to kiss Colby's soft forehead, smiling at him, his tiny ear protectors covering his head.

"You've got this," Morgan said, her voice full of quiet pride that meant the world for Daisy to hear from her big sister.

Robert nodded beside her, his eyes soft. "We're all cheering for you."

Daisy let herself feel it; their support, the love they had for her. It was enough to fuel her through anything.

Riley gave her a tap on the shoulder. "It's time to get ready, Daisy."

The national anthem began to play, and the crowd fell silent. Daisy took her place near her car. As the anthem reached its crescendo, she breathed deeply, letting the moment settle over her. The roar of military jets above rattled her bones as she focused on the race ahead of her.

Jackson's protective presence, the support of her team, the sound of her fans—she was grateful for it all. She knew the road ahead would be difficult. But with everything she had overcome, Daisy was confident in one thing: nothing could stop her today. Or ever.

Riley and the rest of the team secured Daisy into the car. The familiar scent of fuel and exhaust hit Daisy's senses like a jolt of electricity as she settled into the driver's seat. Riley's voice crackled over the radio, confirming that everything was in place. Daisy adjusted her gloves and helmet, ready to fight.

With a deep breath, Daisy closed her eyes for a moment, shutting out the world around her as she focused solely on the task ahead. The cheers of the crowd faded to a dull roar in the background, replaced by the steady thrum of her heartbeat. In this moment, she was more than just carrying on the Kray legacy. She was creating her own—proving that she was not just a driver, but a force to be reckoned with, both on and off the track.

Over the past months, she had learned a lesson that had eluded her up to now. That her freedom came not from evading her vulnerabilities, but from embracing them. Only by facing them could she welcome joy into her life without hesitation. She had to stop living under caution.

Daisy opened her eyes again, feeling an adrenaline rush unlike any other. This was where she belonged, where she felt most alive. She could feel the power within her, the drive to push forward and embrace the road ahead. Come what may.

The final call came through the speakers, clear and sharp, cutting through the air like a command.

"Drivers, start your engines!"

Daisy gripped the wheel tighter, her fingers steady, the weight of the moment settling in her chest. Daisy's car roared to life, the sound vibrating through her body. As the starting line came into focus, the rest of the world faded away. This moment was hers—every twist of the wheel, every acceleration, was a step toward claiming her own destiny. The racetrack was her field of victory, and nothing was going to stop her now.

Epilogue

Lucy Ross sat in the cold Nashville hospital ICU room, her gaze fixed on her brother. Lumen had been unconscious for weeks now, his body tethered to machines that had kept him alive far longer than he should have been.

Lumen's once strong body was now a shell, wrapped in bandages that concealed the damage from the fire. His face, arms, and chest were all covered, making him look like a real-life mummy. The flames had burned not just his skin, but the tissue underneath, leaving him unable to breathe without mechanical assistance. Sepsis had worsened the damage, and it was clear now that he wouldn't make it.

Lucy hoped for a miracle, but today, she signed the papers. The doctor explained that without life support, Lumen would die within hours, possibly minutes. She had fought the decision for so long, but deep down, she knew it was time.

The doctor and nurse left her alone with him, giving her the time to say goodbye. She sat beside his bed, her hands clenched tightly in her lap. As she studied him, the man who was once so full of life, she felt the weight of their shared history. The promises, the betrayals, the rage.

"I'm sorry, Lumen," she murmured, her voice low. She blinked, trying to push the lump in her throat down. "I never thought it would end like this."

Her fingers tapped nervously on the armrest. "We didn't always see eye to eye... but you're still my brother. And I love you."

Her words hung in the air, heavy with the truth she finally accepted.

"I know you weren't perfect, Lumen. But... no one should suffer like you did." Her voice quivered as the weight of it settled on her chest.

Leaning closer, she gently kissed the bandages on his forehead, her lips brushing gently against the fabric. A promise whispered into the stillness. "I'll make sure your technology is perfected. The racing association won't know what hit them. And Agent Turner..." Her eyes darkened, cold and intense. "She won't be able to stop what's coming."

Lucy's eyes blazed with a fierce determination as she spoke.

"As for Daisy Kray..." Her voice deepened, her eyes narrowing with revenge. "She's going to learn about loss."

Lucy hovered above Lumen's forehead for a moment longer. Her mind was already racing, as the future unfolded in her head. There would be vengeance. There would be justice. And this time, she would make sure it was done her way.

The door opened as the doctor and nurse re-entered, awaiting her final approval to proceed. She nodded, steeling herself. Grief clung to her, but it was almost over. Lumen was going to die, and she was going to make sure those responsible for his pain would pay.

Fueled by a toxic blend of love for her brother and a thirst for vengeance, she took a deep breath, her heart pounding with anger and adrenaline, and approached the doctor.

"I'm ready."

The story continues...

Sign up to receive a teaser for the upcoming Book Two and the latest updates at lorizossbooks.com

Acknowledgments

I would like to start by thanking my husband, David, and my parents, Carol and Richard.

I owe a huge debt of gratitude to my editor and fellow author, Cat Margulis whose insight, expertise, and patience have made this book so much stronger. Thank you for pushing me to reach my fullest potential and to embrace a good edit.

To my cover designer and visual marketing guru Jessica Adanich. You are a wonderful friend and have an amazing eye for design. Thank you for bringing the imagery of *Under Caution* to life.

To my voice artists Christy Harst and Jon Smith… Your voices made this story not just heard but felt, and for that, I will always be thankful.

Finally, to all the readers, thank you for supporting this journey. I love action-packed storytelling with compelling characters that allow us to temporarily escape the real world for a thrilling, page-turning adventure, and I hope you enjoyed the ride!

About the Author

Lori Zoss is the author of the suspense romance novel *Under Caution*. A passionate entrepreneur, speaker, and sports fan, Lori brings her unique perspective to her writing, blending thrilling suspense with powerful emotional connections. Lori resides in Cleveland, OH.

Contact Lori at lorizossbooks@gmail.com

You can also connect with Lori Zoss @lorizossauthor on Facebook, Instagram, and YouTube.

Made in the USA
Middletown, DE
21 October 2025